"I'm not leaving until I get what I want."

Something about the set of Blake's jaw made Tillie realize he had the steely will and determination to achieve whatever he put his mind to. And the ruthlessness.

She kept her gaze on his. "Haven't you heard that wise old adage you can't always get what you want?"

Blake glanced at her mouth, then to the swell of her breasts behind her conservatively buttoned cotton shirt, lingering there for a nanosecond before returning his gaze to hers in a lock that ignited something deep inside her body. It was as if his eyes were communicating on an entirely different level—a primal, instinctive level that was as thrilling to her as it was foreign.

No one ever looked at her like...*that.*

As if he were wondering what her mouth would feel like against his. As if he were wondering what she looked like without her practical, no-nonsense clothing. As if he were wondering how she would taste and feel when he put his mouth and tongue to her naked flesh.

Melanie Milburne read her first Harlequin novel at the age of seventeen, in between studying for her final exams. After completing a master's degree in education, she decided to write a novel, and thus her career as a romance author was born. Melanie is an ambassador for the Australian Childhood Foundation and a keen dog lover and trainer. She enjoys long walks in the Tasmanian bush. In 2015 Melanie won the Holt Medallion—a prestigious award honoring outstanding literary talent.

Books by Melanie Milburne

Harlequin Presents

The Temporary Mrs. Marchetti
Unwrapping His Convenient Fiancée
His Mistress for a Week
At No Man's Command

One Night With Consequences

A Ring for the Greek's Baby

Wedlocked!

Wedding Night with Her Enemy

The Ravensdale Scandals

Ravensdale's Defiant Captive
Awakening the Ravensdale Heiress
Engaged to Her Ravensdale Enemy
The Most Scandalous Ravensdale

The Chatsfield

Chatsfield's Ultimate Acquisition
Playboy's Lesson

The Playboys of Argentina

The Valquez Bride
The Valquez Seduction

Visit the Author Profile page at Harlequin.com for more titles.

Melanie Milburne

THE TYCOON'S MARRIAGE DEAL

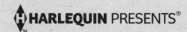

HARLEQUIN PRESENTS®

Recycling programs
for this product may
not exist in your area.

ISBN-13: 978-0-373-06104-4

The Tycoon's Marriage Deal

First North American Publication 2017

Copyright © 2017 by Melanie Milburne

Printed in U.S.A.

THE TYCOON'S
MARRIAGE DEAL

To the Dangerous Liaisons Divas Margie Lawson Advanced Immersion Class in Melbourne 2016—Lauren James, Kristin Meachem, Natasha Daraio, Michelle Somers and of course the marvelous Margie! A special thank you to Kristin's parents, Bill and Anna McKay, who hosted our class in their gorgeous home.

And another special thank you to my dentist, Dr. Jim Rushton, for the use of his cute labradoodle's name!

CHAPTER ONE

IT WAS THE best wedding cake Tillie had ever dec-
orated but now there wasn't going to be a wedding. Her dream wedding. The wedding she had
planned and looked forward to for more years than
she wanted to count. She looked at the triple-tier
wedding cake with the intricate orange blossom
petals she'd taken hours and hours to craft. They
were so darn realistic you could almost smell
them. The finely detailed lacework around the
sides of the cake had all but made her cross-eyed.
She had even given the marzipan bride on the top
of the cake her chestnut hair and pale complexion
and brown eyes, and used a tiny scrap of fabric
from her own wedding dress and veil to make a
replica outfit.

Although…she'd taken a little licence with the
bride's figure and made her look as if she spent
her life in the gym rather than hours in a kitchen

surrounded by yummy cakes that had to be tasted to get the balance of flavours just right.

The groom was exactly like Simon—blond and blue-eyed—although the tuxedo she'd painted on him was now pock-marked with pinholes.

Tillie picked up another dressmaking pin and aimed it at the groom's groin. 'Take that, you cheat.' Who knew marzipan figurines could make such great voodoo dolls? Maybe she could do a side line business for jilted brides, making break-up cakes with an effigy of their ex.

There's a thought…

'Uh-oh.' Joanne, her assistant, came into the kitchen. 'Your favourite male customer is waiting for you. Maybe I should warn him you're in your all-men-are-evil mood.'

Tillie turned from the cake to look at Joanne. 'Which male customer?'

Joanne's eyes sparkled so much they looked as if they belonged on a tiara. 'Mr Chocolate Éclair.'

Tillie could feel her cheeks heating up faster than her fan-forced oven. For the last two weeks, every time that man came into her cake shop he always insisted on being served by her. He always made her blush. And he always wanted the same thing—one of her Belgian chocolate éclairs. She didn't know whether to dislike him for making sport out of her overactive capillaries or for him being able to eat a chocolate éclair a day and not put on a single gram of fat. 'Can't you serve him just this once?'

Joanne shook her head. 'Nope. He wants to speak to you and informs me he won't leave until he does.'

Tillie frowned. 'But I told you I don't want to be interrupted this afternoon. I have three kids' birthday cakes to decorate and I have to squeeze in a visit to Mr Pendleton at the respite centre. I made his favourite marshmallow slice.'

'This guy is not the sort to take no for an answer,' Joanne said. 'Anyway, you should see how clock-stopping gorgeous he looks today. Where on earth does he put all the calories you sell him?'

Tillie turned back to the wedding cake and aimed a pin at the groom's right eye. 'Tell him I'm busy.'

Joanne blew out an I'm-so-over-this breath. 'Look, Tillie, I know Simon jilting you was rough on you, but it's been three months. You have to move on. I think Mr Chocolate Éclair fancies you. He's certainly paying you heaps of attention. Who knows? This might be your chance to get out and party like you've never partied before.'

'Move on? Why should I move on?' Tillie said. 'I'm fine right where I am, thank you very much.

I'm over men.' Three more pins went into marzipan man's manhood. 'Over. Over. Over.'

'But not all men are like—'

'Apart from my dad and Mr Pendleton, men are a waste of time and money and emotion,' Tillie said. When she thought of all the money she'd spent on Simon, helping him with yet another start-up business that ended going belly up. When she thought of all the effort she'd put into their relationship, her patience over his commitment to not have sex before marriage because of his faith, only for him to have an affair with a girl he'd met online.

On a hook-up app.

Grr.

Years Tillie had spent being by his side, putting her own stuff on hold in order to be a good little girlfriend and then good little fiancée. Faithful. Loyal. Devoted.

No. Moving on would mean she would have to trust a man again and that she was never going to do. Not in this lifetime. Not in this century. Not in this geological era.

'So…do you want me to tell Mr Chocolate Éclair to come back some other time?' Joanne said, wincing when she saw all the pins sticking out of Simon.

'No. I'll see him.' Tillie untied her apron,

tossed it to one side and stalked into her small shop front. Mr Chocolate Éclair was standing looking at the cakes and biscuits and slices in the glass cabinet underneath the shop counter. When he turned and made eye contact something zapped her in the chest like a Taser beam. *Zzzztt.* She double-blinked just as she did every time he looked at her. Was it actually possible to have eyes that unusual shade of blue? A light grey-ish-blue with a dark outline around the iris, as if someone had drawn a fine circle with a felt-tip marker. His hair was a rich dark brown with natural highlights as if he had recently spent time in the sun. Clearly not in England, given the summer so far had been dismal even though it was June. His skin was olive toned and tanned and the wrong side of clean-shaven, as if he had been too lazy to pick up a razor that morning. It gave him a rakish air that made her toes curl in her ballet flats.

And he was tall.

So tall he had to stoop when he came in the shop, and even now the top of his head was dangerously close to the light fitting.

But it was his mouth that drew her eyes like a dieter to her cake counter. No matter how hard she tried, Tillie couldn't stop staring at it. The top lip was sculpted and only a shade thinner than the lower one, suggesting his was a mouth that knew all there was to know about sensuality. Even the way it was curved upwards in a smile hinted at a man who was confident and assured of getting his own way in the boardroom and the bedroom or even on a park bench. If there were a blueprint for an international playboy he would be a perfect fit. He was so rampantly masculine he made the models in sexy aftershave ads look like altar boys.

'The usual?' Tillie said, reaching for a set of tongs and a white paper bag.

'Not today.' His voice was so deep it was clear he hadn't been at the back of the queue when the testosterone was handed out. Rich and dark, honey and gravel with a side order of smooth Devonshire cream. His eyes twinkled. 'I'm abstaining from temptation just this once.'

Tillie's cheeks were flaming hot enough to make toffee. 'Can I tempt you with anything else?'

Bad choice of words.

His smile came up a little higher on one side. 'I thought it was time I introduced myself. I'm Blake McClelland.'

The name rang a bell. Not a drawing-room bell. A Big Ben type of bell. Blake McClelland— international playboy, super-successful business-man and renowned financial whizz. McClelland

Park was the name of the country estate Tillie was housesitting for the elderly owner, Mr Pendleton. The estate had been reluctantly sold by Andrew McClelland when his young wife Gwen tragically died, leaving behind a ten-year-old son. The son had certainly done a heck of a lot of growing up. He would be thirty-four now, exactly ten years older than her. 'How can I…erm…help you, Mr McClelland?'

He held out his hand, and, after a brief hesitation, she slipped hers into its slightly calloused cage. The brush of warm male flesh closing around hers was as electrifying as a high-voltage current. The air suddenly became tighter, denser.

'Is there somewhere private we can talk?' he said.

Tillie was rapidly going beyond being able to think, much less talk. Even breathing was proving to be a challenge. Even though she pulled her hand out of his, the sensation of his touch was still travelling through her body like hot tentacles. One of them coiling deep and low in her belly. 'I'm really busy right now so—'

'I won't take up too much of your time.'

She wanted to refuse but she was a businesswoman. Being polite to customers was important to her—even the most annoying ones. What if he wanted to order a speciality cake? Not that she made cakes that big-breasted bunny girls jumped out of, but still. Maybe he wanted her to cater for an event or something. It would be churlish to refuse to speak to him just because he made her feel a little…undone.

'My office is through here,' Tillie said and led the way back to the workroom, every cell of her flesh conscious of him only a few steps behind her.

Joanne looked up from the child's birthday cake she was pretending to decorate with the handmade marzipan toys Tillie had worked on every night for the past week. 'I'll watch over the shop, will I?' she said with a smile so bright it looked as if she were advertising toothpaste.

'Thanks,' Tillie said, opening the office door that led off the workroom. 'We won't be long.'

Well, she'd used to think of it as an office.

Now with Blake McClelland occupying a ridiculous amount of space inside it she rapidly downgraded it to the size of a cake box. A cupcake box.

Tillie waved her hand at the chair in front of her desk. 'Would you like to sit down?'

So I don't have to dislocate my neck to maintain eye contact?

'Ladies first.' Something about the sparkle in his eyes made her think of another context entirely.

She gritted her teeth behind her polite closed-lip smile, and instead of sitting on her own chair, held onto the back of it like a lion tamer about to take on a rogue lion. 'What can I do for you, Mr McClelland?'

'Actually, it's more what I can do for you.' There was an enigmatic quality to his voice and his expression that made the fine hairs on the back of her neck stand up and pirouette.

'Meaning?' Tillie injected enough cool hostility into her tone to have sent a pride of lions scampering for cover, chair or no chair.

Blake glanced at the stack of bills lying on her desk. Three of them were stained with a red stamp marking them as final notices. He would have to be colour blind not to have noticed.

'Local gossip has it you're undergoing a difficult financial period,' he said.

Tillie kept her spine straighter than the ruler on her desk. 'Pardon me if this sounds rude, but I fail to see how my current financial circumstances have anything to do with you.'

His eyes didn't waver from hers. Not even to blink. He reminded her of a marksman who had taken aim, his finger poised on the trigger. 'I noticed the wedding cake on my way in here.'

'Hardly surprising since this is a cake shop,' Tillie said, sounding as tart as the lemon meringue pies she'd made that morning. 'Weddings, parties, anything—it's what I do.'

'I heard about your fiancé getting cold feet on the morning of the wedding,' he said, still holding her gaze with that unnerving target-practice intensity.

'Yes, well, it's hard to keep something like that quiet in a village this size,' she said. 'But again—pardon me for being impolite—what exactly do you want to speak to me about? Because if it's to talk about my ex and his tarty little girlfriend who is barely out of preschool, then you'd better leave right now.'

His smile tilted his mouth in a way that made the base of Tillie's spine tingle and her hand want to rise up and slap him. She curled her fingers into her palms just in case. She was annoyed with herself for allowing him to see how humiliated she was by her ex's choice of partner.

'So here's your chance to get even,' Blake said. 'Pretend to be my fiancée for the next month and I'll take care of those debts for you.'

'Pretend to be your…*what*?'

He picked up the sheaf of papers off her desk and proceeded to read out the amounts owing, whistling through his teeth when he got to the biggest one. He tapped the bills against his other hand and looked at her again with that startlingly direct grey-blue gaze. 'I will pay off your debts and the only payment I want in return is for you to tell your old buddy Jim Pendleton we're engaged.'

Tillie widened her eyes until she thought her eyeballs would pop right out of her head and bounce along the floor like ping-pong balls. 'Are you out of your mind? Pretend to be engaged to *you*? I don't even know you.'

He gave a mock bow. 'Blake Richard Alexander McClelland at your service. Formerly of McClelland Park estate and now on a mission to buy back my ancestral home, which, up until twenty-four years ago, had been in the McClelland family since the mid-seventeen-hundreds.'

Tillie frowned. 'But why don't you make an offer to Mr Pendleton? He's been talking about selling since he had a stroke two months ago.'

'He won't sell it to me.'

'Why not?'

His eyes continued to hold hers but this time there was a devilish glint. 'Apparently my reputation as a love-them-and-leave-them playboy has annoyed him.'

Tillie could well imagine Blake McClelland had done some serious damage to a few hearts in his time. Now she realised why he'd seemed familiar the first time he'd come into her shop. She recalled reading something recently about him at a wild party in Vegas involving three burlesque dancers. He had a fast-living lifestyle that would certainly be at odds with someone as old and conservative as Jim Pendleton, whose only misdemeanours in eighty-five years were a couple of parking fines. 'But Mr Pendleton would never believe you and I were a couple. We're total opposites.'

His smile was crooked. 'But that's the point— you're exactly the type of girl Jim would want me to fall in love with and settle down.'

As if that would ever happen.

Tillie knew she wasn't responsible for any shat- tered mirrors about the place, but neither would she be asked to model a bikini on a catwalk. Her girl-next-door looks wouldn't stop a clock or even a wristwatch. Not even an egg timer. The likeli- hood of attracting someone as heart-stoppingly handsome and suave and sophisticated as Blake McClelland was as likely as her becoming a size zero. But she didn't know whether to be insulted or grateful. Right now, the thought of paying off her debts was more tempting than a whole tray of Belgian chocolate éclairs. Two trays. And even better, it would send a middle finger in the air to her ex. 'But won't Mr Pendleton suspect some- thing if we suddenly come out as a couple? He might be elderly and suffering from a stroke, but he's not stupid.'

'The old man's a romance tragic,' Blake said. 'He was married fifty-nine years before his wife died. He fell in love with her within ten minutes of meeting her. He'll be thrilled to see you move on from your ex. He talked about you non-stop—called you his little guardian angel. He said you were minding his house and his dog and visiting him every day. That's how I came up with the plan. I can see the headlines now.' He put his fingers up in air quotes. *'"Bad boy tamed by squeaky clean girl next door."'* His grin was straight off a cosmetic orthodontist's website. 'It's win-win.'

Tillie gave him a look that would have soured her shop's week's supply of milk. 'I hate to put a dent in that massive ego of yours, but my answer is an emphatic, irreversible no.'

'I don't expect you to sleep with me.'

Tillie didn't care for the way he said it as if she was being a gauche fool for thinking otherwise. Why didn't he expect her to sleep with him? Was she *that* hideous? 'Good, because I wouldn't do it even if you paid those debts fifty gazillion times over.'

Something about the spark of light in his eyes sent a shuddering tremor over the floor of her belly. His slanted smile was star student of charm school. 'Although, if you ever change your mind I'll be happy to get down to business.'

Business? Tillie dug her fingers into the back of her office chair so hard she thought her knuckles would explode. She wanted to slap that I-can-have-you-any-time-I-want-you smile off his face. But another part—a secret, private part—wanted him. Wanted. Wanted. *Wanted* him. 'I'm *not* going to change my mind.'

He picked up a pen off her desk, tossed it in the air and deftly caught it in one hand. 'And when the time comes to end it, I will allow you the privilege of dumping me.'

'Big of you.'

'I'm not being magnanimous,' he said. 'I don't want to be run out of town by a bunch of villagers wielding baseball bats.'

Tillie wished she had a baseball bat handy right now to beat her resolve back into shape. But the chance to let her ex know she could land a guy was proving a little hard to resist.

And not just any old guy.

Someone rich and gorgeous and sexy as sin on a sugar-coated stick. It was only for a month. How hard could it be? Her thoughts were seesawing in her head. *Do it. Don't. Do it. Don't.*

'Think about it overnight,' Blake said, apparently undaunted because his smile didn't falter. 'I want a walk around the Park some time. For old times' sake.'

'I'd have to ask Mr Pendleton if that's okay with him.'

'Fine.' He took a business card from his wallet and handed it to her. 'My contact details. I've checked in at the bed and breakfast down the road.'

Tillie took the card from him, desperately trying not to touch his fingers. Those long tanned fingers. Those long tanned masculine fingers. She couldn't stop thinking about how those fingers would feel on her skin…on her body. On her breasts. Between her legs.

She gave herself a concussion-inducing mental slap. Why was she thinking about intimate stuff like that? The only person who'd ever touched her between the legs—apart from herself—was her gynaecologist.

'I wouldn't have thought cottage flowers and cosy fireplaces and fancy china teacups would be to your taste,' Tillie said.

Blake's eyes glinted again. 'I don't plan to stay there long.'

What was he hinting? That he would be staying with her? Tillie inched up her chin, trying to ignore the way the backs of her knees were fizzing in reaction to the satirical light in his gaze. 'I'm sure you'll find much more suitable accommodation for your…erm…needs in the next town.'

The less you think about his 'needs', the better.

'Perhaps, but I'm not leaving this village until I get what I want.' Something about the set of his jaw made her realise he had the steely will and determination to achieve whatever he put his mind to. And the ruthlessness.

She kept her gaze on his. 'Haven't you heard that wise old adage you can't always get what you want?'

Blake glanced at her mouth, then to the swell of her breasts behind her conservatively buttoned cotton shirt, lingering there for a nanosecond before returning his gaze to hers in a lock that ignited something deep inside her body. It was as if his eyes were communicating on an entirely different level—a primal, instinctive level that was as thrilling to her as it was foreign.

No one ever looked at her like…*that*.

As if he were wondering what her mouth would feel like against his. As if he were wondering what she looked like without her practical, no-nonsense clothing. As if he were wondering how she would taste and feel when he put his mouth and tongue to her naked flesh.

Even Simon had never given her The Look. The I-want-to-have-bed-wrecking-sex-with-you-right-now look. She'd always put it down to the fact he'd staunchly committed to celibacy, but now she wondered if the chemistry had ever been there. Their kisses and cuddles seemed somehow…vanilla. Unlike her, Simon had had sex previously as a young teenager, but he'd felt so guilty he'd made a pledge not to do it again until he was married. They'd occasionally petted but never without clothes. The only pleasure she'd had during the last eight years had been with herself.

But nothing about Blake McClelland was vanilla. He was dark chocolate fudge and tantalising, willpower-destroying temptation. She couldn't imagine him being celibate for eight minutes, let alone eight years. Which made it all the more laughable he wanted her to pretend to be his fiancée.

Who would ever believe it?

'Just for the record,' Blake said in a voice so deep it made Simon's baritone sound like a boy soprano, 'I *always* get what I want.'

Tillie suppressed an involuntary shiver at the streak of ruthless determination in his tone. But she kept her expression in starchy schoolmistress mode. 'Here's the thing, Mr McClelland. I'm not the sort of girl to be toyed with for a man's entertainment. That's what this is about, isn't it? You're a bored playboy who's looking for the next challenge. You thought you could waltz in here and brandish your big fat bank account and get me to fall on my knees with gratitude, didn't you?'

His eyes did that twinkling, glinting thing. 'Not on our first date. I like to have something to look forward to.'

Tillie could feel her blush shoot to the roots of her hair. She almost expected it to be singed right off her scalp. She could barely speak for the anger vibrating through her body.

Or maybe it wasn't anger...

Maybe it was a far more primitive emotion rushing through her in blazing, electrifying streaks. Desire. A pulse-throbbing sexual energy that left no part of her untouched. It was as if her blood were injected with its bubbling hot urgency. She shot him a glare as deadly as one of her metal cake skewers. 'Get out of my shop.'

Blake tapped his index finger on the stack of bills on her desk. 'It won't be your shop for much longer if these aren't seen to soon. Give me a call when you've changed your mind.'

Tillie lifted one of her brows as if she were channelling a heroine in a period drama. '*When?* Don't you mean *if*?'

His eyes held hers in an iron will against iron will tug of war, making her heart skip a beat. Two beats. Possibly three. If she'd been on a cardiac ward they would have called a Code Blue.

'You know you want to.'

Tillie wasn't sure they were still talking about the money. There was a dangerous undercurrent rippling in the air. Air she couldn't quite get into her lungs. But then he picked up his business card, which she'd placed on her desk earlier, and, reaching across the small space the desk offered, slid it into the right breast pocket of her shirt. At no point did he touch her, but it felt as if he had stroked her breast with one of those long, clever fingers. Her breast fizzed as if a firework were trapped inside the cup of her bra.

'Call me,' he said.

'You'll be waiting a long time.'

His smile was confident. Brazenly confident. I've-got-this-in-the-bag confident. 'You think?'

That was the whole darn trouble. Tillie couldn't think. Not while he was standing there dangling temptation in front of her. She'd always prided herself on her resolve, but right now it felt as if her resolve had rolled over and was playing dead.

She owed a lot of money. More money than she earned in a year. Way more. She had to pay her father and stepmother back the small loan they'd given her because as missionaries living abroad they were living on gifts and tithes as it was. Mr Pendleton had offered to help her but it didn't sit well with her to take money off him when he had already been incredibly generous by allowing her to stay at McClelland Park rent-free and to use his kitchen for baking when she ran out of time at the shop. Besides, he would need all his money and more if he didn't sell McClelland Park, because an old Georgian property that size needed constant and frighteningly expensive maintenance.

But to take money off Blake McClelland in exchange for a month pretending to be his fiancée was a step into territory so dangerous she would need to be immediately measured for a straitjacket. Even if he didn't expect her to sleep with him she would have to act as if she were. She would have to touch him, hold hands or have him—*gulp*—kiss her for the sake of appearances.

'Good day, McClelland,' Tillie said, as sternly as if she were dismissing an impertinent boy from the staffroom.

Blake was almost out of her office when he turned around at the door to look back at her. 'Oh, one other thing.' He fished in his trouser pocket and took out a velvet ring box and tossed it to her desk to land on top of her stack of bills with unnerving accuracy. 'You'll be needing this.'

And without stopping to see her open the box, he turned and left.

CHAPTER TWO

JOANNE CAME INTO the office before Tillie had time to pick her dropped jaw up off the desk, much less the ring box. 'Oh. My. God. Is that what I think it is?' she said.

Tillie stared at the box as if it were a detonator device. 'I'm not going to open it.'

I'm not. I'm not. I'm not.

Even though her finger still felt horribly empty after three years of wearing an engagement ring. Three years and another five before that wearing a friendship/commitment ring. But she had a feeling Blake's ring wouldn't look anything like the humble little quarter-carat diamond Simon had purchased. Actually, Simon hadn't purchased it. She'd put it on her credit card and he was meant to repay her but somehow never did. Another clue he hadn't truly loved her.

Why hadn't she realised that until now?

'Well, if you don't want it, give it to me,' Joanne said. 'I'm not against gorgeous men buying me expensive jewellery. What did he want to speak to you about?'

'You wouldn't believe me if I told you.'

'Try me.'

Tillie let out a gust of a breath. 'He wants to settle all of my debts in exchange for me pretending to be his fiancée for a month.'

'You're right. I don't believe you.'

'He's the most arrogant man I've ever met,' Tillie said. 'The hide of him marching in here expecting me to say yes to such a ridiculous farce. Who would believe it anyway? Me engaged to someone like him?'

Joanne's smooth brow crinkled in thought. 'I don't know… I think you're a little hard on yourself. I mean, I know you're not big on fashion but if you wore a bit more colour and a bit of make-up you'd look awesome. And you've got great boobs but you never show any cleavage.'

Tillie sat down with a thump on her desk chair. 'Yes, well, Simon didn't like it when women paraded their assets.'

And how could I have spent money on clothes and make-up while saving for the wedding?

'Simon was born in the wrong century,' Joanne said with a roll of her eyes. 'I reckon you're better off without him. He never even took you out dancing, for pity's sake. You deserve someone much more dynamic than him. He's too bland. Blake McClelland, on the other hand, is capital D dynamite.'

Blake McClelland was too darn everything.

Tillie eyed the ring box again, curling her fingers into her palms like hooks to stop herself reaching for it. 'I'm going to take it to Mrs Fisher's second-hand shop.'

Joanne couldn't have look more shocked than if she'd said she was going to flush it down the toilet. 'Surely you're not serious?'

Tillie left the ring box where it was and pushed back from her desk. 'I'm deadly serious.'

Blake drove the few kilometres out from the village to his family's estate in rural Wiltshire. He had driven past a few times over the years after leaving flowers at his mother's grave at the cemetery in the village, but he hadn't been able to bring himself to stop and survey the estate in any detail. To stare at the home that used to belong in his family had always been too painful, like jabbing at a wound that had never properly healed.

The bank had repossessed the estate after his father's breakdown. As a ten-year-old child it had been devastating enough to lose his mother, but to see his father crumple emotionally, to cease to function other than on a level not much higher than breathing, was terrifying. His mother's death from a brain aneurysm had shattered him and his father. The cruel unexpectedness of it. The blunt shock of having her laughing and smiling one minute and then slurring her speech and then stumbling and falling the next. Ten days in hospital on life support until the doctors had given them the devastating news there was no longer any hope.

The mother he'd adored and who had made his and his father's life so perfect and happy had gone.

Irretrievably gone.

But somehow some measure of childhood resilience had kicked in and he'd become the parent during the long years of his father's slow climb out of the abyss of despair. His dad had never remarried or re-partnered. Hadn't even dated.

But after his dad's recent health scare, Blake was determined to put this one wrong thing right; no matter what the cost or the effort. McClelland Park was the key to his father's full recovery.

He knew it in his blood. He knew it in his bones. He knew it at a cellular level.

His dad felt enormous guilt and shame about losing the property that had been passed down through the generations. Blake suspected his dad's inability to move on with his life was tied up in the loss of the estate. His dad would literally die a slow and painful death without it being returned to him.

It was up to Blake to get McClelland Park back and get it back he would.

He smiled when he thought of Matilda Toppington. Colour him every shade of confident but he knew he had this in the bag with a big satin ribbon tied around it. She was exactly the woman for the job. Old man Pendleton wouldn't stop gushing about her—how kind and considerate she was, all the charitable work she did in the local community, the way she took care of everyone. He'd seen it himself each time he'd been in the shop. Freebies for the kids, special treats for the elderly, home deliveries for the infirm. Tillie was such a do-gooder; he was surprised she hadn't sprouted a pair of wings and didn't carry a harp under her arm. When pressed on the aborted wedding, the old man had more or less hinted he was relieved it hadn't gone ahead. Apparently so was everyone else in the village, although, according to Maude Rosethorne at the bed and breakfast, most weren't game enough to say it to Tillie's face.

But Blake was certain Tillie would say yes to

him about the pretend engagement, if not yes to sleeping with him. When had a woman ever said no? He was the package most women wanted: wealth, status, looks and skill in bed. Besides, he was giving her the perfect tool to get back at her ex by showing off a new lover.

And becoming Tillie Toppington's lover was something he was seriously tempted to do. From the first moment he'd met her gaze he'd been intrigued by her. She wasn't his usual type but he was up for a change. The way she'd blushed when he'd first spoken to her made him do it all the more. She pretended to dislike him but he knew she was interested. All the signs were there. She was responding to him the way he responded to her—with good old-fashioned, clothes-ripping lust.

Okay, so call him vain, but no woman had ever complained about not having a good time in his bed. Not that he let them spend much time in it. He had a policy of no longer than a month. After that things got tricky. Women started measuring him for a morning suit. They started dropping hints about engagement rings or started dragging their heels while going past jewellery shop windows.

The estate came into view and a boulder landed in Blake's gut. The silver-birch-lined driveway leading to the house brought back a rush of memories. The screaming siren of the ambulance as his mother was rushed to hospital. The drive home with his father, the night his mother died. The empty front passenger seat where his mother should have been sitting. How he had stared at that seat with his eyes burning and his stomach churning and his head pounding with a silent scream.

The horrible silence.

The silence that gouged a hole in his chest that had never properly closed. If he closed his eyes he could still hear the crunch of the car tyres on the gravel on that last drive out twenty-four years ago, that and the sound of his father's quiet but no less heart-bludgeoning sobbing.

Blake braked but didn't turn into the driveway. After a slow drive past his memories, he put his foot down and drove on with a roar of the engine.

He would wait until he heard from Tillie before he finally came home.

Tillie walked into her office to put another bill on the pile. She had kept out of there for most of the day, determined to resist peeking at the ring. And to avoid looking at the stack of bills on her desk. She put the overdue florist notice on top of the others and eyed the ring box as if it were a cockroach in cake batter. 'You think I'm going to look at you, don't you? You've been sitting there all day just waiting for me to break.'

Taking money from Mrs Fisher's pawnshop for Blake's ring was proving a little tricky for Tillie's conscience. He had given it to her but it was hardly a no-strings gift. There were conditions attached. Conditions that involved what exactly? He'd said *pretend* to be his fiancée. What would that involve? Hanging out with him? Would hanging out include kissing him? Touching him?

Him touching her?

He'd said sleeping with him wasn't mandatory but she'd seen the way his eyes darkened every time they met hers. Darkened and smouldered and made her body feel as if she were sitting too close to a fire. Naked.

Maybe she should have discussed the terms with him. Sussed out some of the details before she flatly refused. The bills weren't going away—they were mounting up like a croquembouche cake.

Tillie sat down, and after a moment, began tapping her fingers on the desk. 'It's no good looking at me like that. You could be the identical twin of the Hope Diamond and I still wouldn't look at you.'

After another long moment, she gently nudged the box, moving it a millimetre away as if she were pushing away a crumb. The box was plush velvet. Rich velvet. Luxury jeweller's velvet.

Hours had passed since Blake had given the ring to her, but she couldn't help thinking about how that box had been in his trouser pocket right next to his...

Tillie snatched her hand back and tucked it in her lap, eyeballing the ring box as if it were a poisonous viper sitting on her desk. 'Thought you had me there, didn't you?'

Joanne came into the office. 'Who on earth are you talking to?' she said and then glanced at the ring on the desk, a smile breaking over her face. 'Ah.'

'What do you mean "ah"?' Tillie said, scowling.

Joanne's eyes were doing the tiara thing again. 'You want to *so* bad.'

'No, I don't.' Tillie folded her arms.

'Not even a little peek?' Joanne's hand reached for the box.

'Don't touch it!'

Joanne's eyebrows went up and her smile widened so far it nearly fell off her face. 'I thought you were going to take it to Mrs Fisher's?'

'Changed my mind.'

'Because Mrs Fisher is the village's version of Facebook?'

'Exactly.'

Joanne perched on the edge of the desk, her eyes on the ring. 'I wonder if he paid a lot for it?'

'I. Do. Not. Care.'

'Maybe it's not a real diamond,' Joanne said in a musing tone. 'Some of those zircon ones look pretty amazing. You'd never know it wasn't the real thing.'

'I hardly think Blake McClelland is the type of man to buy a girl a zircon instead of a diamond,' Tillie said.

Joanne's twinkling eyes met Tillie's. 'True.'

Tillie frowned. 'Why are you looking at me like that?'

'How am I looking at you?' Joanne's tone was so innocent it would have made an angel's sound evil.

'Don't you have work to do?' Tillie said with an I'm-your-boss arch of her brow.

Joanne's cheeky smile didn't back down. 'Best not look at it, then. You might want to keep it.' And giving a little finger wave, she left.

Tillie rolled her chair closer to the desk and picked up the ring box. She turned it over and over as if she were about to solve a Rubik's Cube. What harm would one little peek do? No one would know she'd taken a look. She cautiously lifted the lid and then gasped. Inside was a stunning handcrafted ring that was set in a Gatsby era style. It wasn't look-at-me huge but its finely crafted setting gave it an air of priceless beauty. There were a central diamond and two smaller ones either side of it, and a collection of tiny diamonds surrounding them. The sides of the ring were inset with more glittering tiny diamonds.

Tillie had seen some engagement rings in her time but none as beautiful as this. Hopelessly impractical, of course. She couldn't imagine thrusting her hands into pastry while wearing it but, oh, how gorgeous was it?

You can't keep it.

Right now Tillie didn't want to listen to her conscience. She wanted to slip that ring over her finger and step out and parade it in the village to make sure everyone saw it winking there.

Take that, you cheating low-life ex. See what sort of calibre of man I can hook?

No one would be casting her pitying looks then. No one would be whispering behind their hands when she walked past them or into their shops, or asking each other *sotto voce*, *'How do you think she's holding up?'* and, *'Doesn't she look a little peaky to you?'* or, *'I never thought Simon was right for her anyway.'*

She took the ring out of the velvet-lined box and held it in the palm of her hand.

Go on. Put it on. See if it fits.

Tillie picked up the ring and, taking a deep breath, slipped it over her ring finger. It was a little snug but it fitted her finger better than the one Simon had 'given' her. She kept staring at the ring's dazzling beauty, wondering how much it was worth. Wondering if she should take it off right this second before she got too attached to it. She had never worn anything so gorgeous. Her late mother hadn't had much jewellery to speak of because she and Tillie's dad were always so frugal over money in order to help others less fortunate. They hadn't even bought an engagement ring but instead donated what they would have spent to their church's missionary fund. Some of that social ethic had rubbed off on Tillie even though she didn't even remember her mother because she'd died just hours after Tillie was born. But this was the sort of ring to be passed down generations from mothers to daughter to granddaughters and great-granddaughters.

Although Tillie had grown up in a loving home, largely due to her kind stepmother who was the antithesis of the wicked stepmother stereotype, she had still longed to belong to someone, to build a life together and raise a family. To have that special someone to be there for her, as her stepmother was there for her father, and

Tillie's mother before her. Prior to being jilted, she'd been a fully signed up member to the Love Makes the World Go Around Club.

Breaking up with Simon after so long together shattered her dream of happy ever after. She had been cast adrift like a tiny dinghy left bobbing alone in the ocean without a rudder or even an anchor. Three months on, it still felt a little odd to go out to dinner or visit the cinema on her own but she was determined to learn how to do it without feeling like a loser. It felt a little weird to be cooking a meal for one person but she was working on that, too—besides, she could do with a little less eating.

Now she was a fully paid up member of the Single and Loving It Club.

Well…maybe the Single and Still Getting Used to It Club was more appropriate.

But she would learn to love it even if it damn near killed her.

Tillie was about to take off the ring when her phone rang. She picked it up to see the number on the screen was the respite facility Mr Pendleton was staying in. 'Hello?'

'Tillie, it's Claire Reed, one of the senior nurses on staff,' a woman's voice said. 'I'm afraid Mr Pendleton's had a nasty fall coming out of the bathroom earlier today. He's okay now but he's asking to see you. Can you come in when you get a chance?'

Tillie's stomach pitched. Mr Pendleton was already so frail; another fall would set him back even further. 'Oh, the poor darling. Of course, I'll come in straight away—I was on my way in any case.'

She hung up from the call and went to snatch up her bag and cardigan off the back of the chair, but then she noticed the ring still on her finger. She went to pull it off but it refused to come back over her knuckle. Panic started beating in her chest as frantically as her food mixer whipping up egg whites for meringues.

She had to get it off!

She tugged it again, almost bruising her knuckle in the process. But the more she tugged, the more her knuckle swelled until the joint was almost as big as a Californian walnut. And throbbing painfully as if she had full-blown rheumatoid arthritis.

Tillie dashed into the workroom and shoved her hand under the cold-water tap, liberally soaping up the joint to see if it would help. It didn't. The ring had apparently decided it quite liked its new home on her finger and was staying put, thank you very much. She let out a rarely used swear word and grabbed some hand lotion. She greased up her finger but the more she pushed against her knuckle, the more it throbbed.

She gave up. She would have to leave it and get it off later when the swelling of her knuckle went down.

When Tillie got to the respite centre, the geriatrician on duty informed her that, along with some cuts and bruises and a black eye, Mr Pendleton was also suffering some slight memory confusion as a result of the fall and that he might well have had another mini stroke, which might have caused the loss of balance. She told Tillie not to be unduly concerned about the fact he was acting a little irritable and grumpy but to go along with whatever the old man said so as to not stress him too much.

When Tillie entered his room, Mr Pendleton was sitting propped up in bed looking sorry for himself with an aubergine-coloured bruise on his left cheek and a black eye. He had a white plaster bandage over a cut on his forehead where his head —according to the doctor—had bumped against the toilet bowl.

'Oh, Mr Pendleton.' Tillie rushed to his bedside and carefully took his crêpe-paper-thin hand in hers. 'Are you all right? The doctor said you'd had a bad fall. What have you been doing to yourself? You look like you've gone a couple of rounds with a boxer and a sumo wrestler.'

The old man glowered at her instead of his usual smile of welcome. 'I don't know why you bother visiting an old goat like me. I'm ready for the scrap heap. If I were a dog they would've put me down long ago like the vet did with poor old Humphrey.'

'I come because I care about you,' Tillie said. 'Everyone in the village cares about you. Now tell me what happened.'

He plucked at the hem of the light cotton blanket covering him as if it were annoying him. 'I don't remember what happened. One minute I was upright and the next I was on the floor… I'm all right apart from a bit of a headache.'

'Well, as long as you're okay now, that's the main thing,' Tillie said. 'I would've brought Truffles in to see you but I haven't been home yet. I came straight from work.'

Truffles was Mr Pendleton's chocolate-coloured labradoodle who had not yet progressed from puppyhood even though she was now two years old. Tillie had helped name her when Mr Pendleton had bought the puppy to keep him company after his old golden retriever Humphrey had to be euthanised. But Truffles was nothing like the sedate and portly Humphrey, who had lain in front of the fireplace and snored for hours, only waking for meals and a slow mooch outside for calls of nature. Truffles moved like a dervish on crack and had a penchant for chewing things such as shoes and handbags and sunglasses—all of them Tillie's. Truffles dug so many holes in the garden it looked as if she were drilling for oil. She brought in sticks and leaves as playthings and hid them under the sofa cushions, along with— on one memorable occasion—a dead bird. Not recently dead. Maggot-stage dead.

Tillie often brought Truffles in to see Mr Pendleton, but not unless she'd exhausted the dog with a long walk and some ball play first. A bull in a china shop would look like a butterfly compared to that crazy mutt.

Mr Pendleton's gaze went to Tillie's hands where they were holding his and spied the diamond ring glittering brighter than a lighthouse beacon. His faded blue eyes suddenly narrowed. 'Don't tell me what's his name—Scott? Shaun?— has come crawling back?' he said.

Tillie's heart was giving a rather credible impression of having a serious medical event. She glanced at the resuscitation gear above Mr Pendleton's bed for reassurance. Why hadn't she thought to put on a pair of gloves? Although, given it was summer it might have looked a little odd. No more odd than wearing an engagement ring that looked as though it cost more than it would to feed a small nation. 'Erm… Simon? No. Someone…else gave it to me.'

Mr Pendleton's frown deepened and he leaned forward like a detective staring down a prevaricating suspect. 'Who?'

'Erm…'

'Speak up, girl,' he said. 'You know I'm a little hard of hearing. Who gave you that ring? It looks like a good one.'

Tillie swallowed. 'B-Blake McClelland.'

Mr Pendleton's bushy eyebrows shot up like caterpillars zapped with an electrode. Then he started laughing. Not chuckling laughing, but the sort of laughing you heard at an Irish comedy festival. He rocked back and forth against his banked-up pillows, eyes squinted, and guffawed for so long she began to worry he would do himself an injury, like rupture his voice box or something. 'Now that's just what I needed to lift my spirits out of the doldrums,' he said. 'Did the doctor put you up to it? They always say laughter's the best medicine. You've done me a power of good, Tillie. You, engaged to Blake McClelland? Funniest thing I've heard in years.'

Tillie shifted her lips from side to side, annoyed that he found it so amusing and unlikely someone like Blake would ever propose to her. Why didn't he think she was good enough for Blake?

Was it because she wasn't exciting enough? Not attractive enough? She might not be classically beautiful, but so far no travelling circus had ever asked her to sit in a tent and charged an entry fee for people to gawp at her.

'No, this has nothing to do with the doctor. It's not a joke. It's true. Blake did give it to me. He asked me to—'

'You're a bit late for April Fool's day.' Mr Pendleton was still laughing. 'I might be a bit muddled in my head but I know it's June.'

The stubborn streak Tillie had worked for years to suppress while she was with Simon came back with a vengeance. Gone was the submissive any-thing-you-say-dear girl. In her place was Tena-cious Tillie. She would *make* Mr Pendleton believe she was engaged to Blake. She would make every-one believe it. No one would think her not up to the task of hooking a hot man after she was done.

'We met a couple of weeks ago when he came into the shop. It was love at first sight. On both sides. It was instant, just like in the movies. He's the love of my life. I know it as sure as I'm sit-ting here telling you. He asked me to marry him and I said yes.'

Mr Pendleton stopped laughing and began to frown instead. 'Look, I might be nearly ninety but I'm no old fool in his dotage. You're not the sort of girl who falls for men like him. You're too conservative to have your head turned by such a handsome devil. And he's not the sort to fall for someone like you.'

Pride made Tillie sit stiffly in her chair while her ego slunk away to hide weeping in the corner. *Too conservative?* She had only been conservative for all these years because Simon had insisted on it. Sure, she might not be going to rush off to steal cars or snatch purses off old ladies any time soon, but neither was she planning to sit at home every night in front of a PG movie with forty-seven cats for company. 'What do you mean Blake wouldn't fall for someone like me? He's in love with me and wants to marry me.' *What's wrong with me?*

'Tillie…' Mr Pendleton gave her hand a little pat. 'You're a good girl. You always colour between the lines. Blake McClelland on the other hand is too much for an old-fashioned girl like you to handle. You'd never be able to tame him. And you're too sensible to even try.'

Old-fashioned. *Sensible.* She would show everyone just how 'old-fashioned and sensible' she was—including Blake McClelland. 'Maybe I have already tamed him,' Tillie said, pulling her hand away. 'Maybe he's sick of being a playboy and wants to settle down and have babies. That's why he wants to buy McClelland Park because—'

'He wants to buy McClelland Park because he's filthy rich and thinks he can open his wallet and get anything he likes,' Mr Pendleton said. 'It's time that man learned a lesson. And you, my dear, are not the one to teach him. Stay away from him. You've already had your heart broken once.'

'But I love him,' Tillie said, mentally crossing her fingers for all the lies spouting out of her mouth. 'I really do. He's so much more exciting and interesting than Simon. I can't believe I ever fancied myself in love with Simon now. Blake is romantic and attentive in a way Simon never was nor ever could be. He makes me feel things I've never felt before. I—'

'Have you slept with him?' The old man's gaze was as direct as a laser pointer at a scientific meeting.

Tillie opened and closed her mouth, her cheeks feeling so hot she was sure they were going to scald the skin right off her face. 'That's a rather personal question to—'

'Has he moved in with you?'

'Erm…would that be okay if he did?'

Yikes! What are you doing?

Mr Pendleton was still looking at her as a cop

did a sneaky suspect. 'He's not the marrying sort, you know, and good girls like you always want marriage. I'm not saying he isn't charming. He is. Just about every nurse in this place goes into a swoon when he comes in here. He's only put that ring on your finger to sleep with you. As soon as he's done that he'll be off in search of the next conquest, you mark my words.'

The nurse popped her head around the door. 'Everything all right, Mr Pendleton?'

'Tillie fancies herself in love with Blake Mc-Clelland,' he said with a snort. 'Says she's engaged to him. And you think I'm the one who's confused.'

The nurse glanced at Tillie with wide did-I-just-hear-that-correctly? eyes. 'Blake McClelland and...*you*?'

Tillie's ego had had just about enough bludgeoning for one day. 'Yes. He asked me yesterday. He's been coming into the shop every day for the last couple of weeks and we hit it off. I know it's a bit of a whirlwind, but when you've met the right one you just know.'

'Oh, Tillie, I'm so thrilled for you. Everyone will be when they hear the news,' the nurse said. 'When are you getting married?'

'Erm...we haven't set a date yet but—'

'It's fabulous you've found someone. Really fabulous. We've all been so worried about you.'

The nurse led Tillie out of the room and softly closed the door. 'Don't listen to Mr Pendleton. He's still a little out of sorts from his fall. He'll be delighted for you in a few days. Give me a look at that ring. Gosh, isn't it gorgeous? Much nicer than he-whose-name-is-not-to-be-mentioned.'

'Yes. I'm very happy.'

Who knew how easy it was to lie?

'I have a theory about playboys,' the nurse said. 'They make the best husbands in the end. They get all that running around out of their system and then they settle down.'

Tillie was pretty sure Blake McClelland had no intention of settling down and certainly not with someone like her. What was she going to do now? Mr Pendleton might doubt her engagement but the nurse clearly didn't. It would be all over the village within hours. Tillie was effectively engaged to Blake even though she'd adamantly told him no. She could almost see his sardonic I've-got-you-where-I-want-you smile.

She slipped out of the respite facility and back to her car. The ring was still stuck on her finger as if some mischievous supernatural forces had conspired against her.

How was she going to face Blake now?

* * *

Blake came back to the bed and breakfast after tidying his mother's grave at the cemetery. He hadn't stayed in a B&B since he was a kid on one of the rare holidays his father took him on. But the cottage had a nice vibe—an old-world charm about it that made his business mind spark with ideas.

However, he didn't get a chance to discuss a business proposal when he entered the cottage's rose-framed front door because Maude Rosethorne was standing there with a broad smile on her face.

'Congratulations, Mr McClelland,' she said. 'We're all so excited with the news of Tillie and you getting engaged. It's the most romantic thing ever. It's all over the village. We didn't even know you two knew each other and now you're getting married!'

Blake had counted on that ring changing Tillie's mind. What girl could resist a rock like that? It was worth a minor fortune, but he wasn't quibbling over the expense—no expense was too much in his quest to get back his family property. 'Thank you,' he said. 'What's that old saying? When you've met the right one you just know?'

'She's a wonderful girl—but you don't need me to tell you that,' Mrs Rosethorne said. 'Everyone loves Tillie. We've all been so worried about her after Simon jilted her. I suppose she's told you all about that? Terrible, just terrible to leave her to face all the guests like that. He sent a text message. A text message! Didn't have the backbone to see her face to face. He's no longer welcome around these parts, let me tell you. No one gets to break our Tillie's heart without all of us in the village having something to say about it.'

Blake went to his room feeling relieved he'd offered Tillie the chance to end their relationship once his goal of securing McClelland Park was achieved. He didn't want his father to feel unwelcome when he finally moved back home. Blake wasn't interested in breaking any hearts. Tillie hadn't bothered to disguise her instant dislike of him—a novel experience for him, as he usually had no trouble winning women over within seconds of meeting them.

Her reaction to him amused him. He liked nothing more than a challenge, and cute little Matilda Toppington was nothing if not an Olympic-standard challenge. She was feisty and quick-witted and sharp-tongued with a body as delectable as the cakes and slices in her shop cabinet. Not beautiful in the traditional sense, but with the sort of understated looks that held a compelling fascination for him. For years he'd been surrounded by stunning-looking women, so much so they were starting to look the same. Even their personalities seemed similar—or maybe that was his fault for only ever dating a certain type.

But when Tillie hitched her chin and glared down her uptilted nose at him with those flashing nutmeg-brown eyes, he couldn't help thinking how unique she was, how refreshing and unaffected. Her mouth was on the fuller side with an adorable little Cupid's bow. For the last couple of weeks he'd been fantasising about kissing those soft and pliable-looking lips. She might not like him but he knew raw physical attraction when he saw it. Such crackling chemistry would make their 'engagement' all the more entertaining. That was probably why she'd decided to run with the engagement in spite of telling him to take his offer and get out of Dodge before dawn. And why not? A fling between them wouldn't be hurting anyone.

He allowed himself a congratulatory smile.

The ring had been the bait and she'd snapped it up just as he'd planned.

Tillie was walking Truffles around the lake in front of McClelland Park still wondering how on earth she was going to face Blake. Her phone had been running hot ever since she'd left the respite centre. When she went back to her shop, she'd explained to Joanne what had happened, but, instead of being upset on her behalf, Joanne had seemed inordinately thrilled, spouting such idiotic statements as 'it's meant to be' and something about 'fate's meddling hand'. Joanne had even gone on to say how she thought Tillie was secretly in love with Blake but hadn't yet admitted it to herself.

In love with Blake McClelland?

What a flipping joke. Tillie had been so put off by her assistant's reaction she'd turned her phone off rather than face the barrage of hearty congratulations from everyone else.

Everyone apart from Mr Pendleton, that was.

How soon before Blake found out on the village gossip network? Should she text him or call him? She had his card somewhere...or had she thrown it out?

Truffles suddenly pricked up her ears and looked to the front wrought-iron gates where a low-slung sports car was turning into the driveway. It came up through the avenue of silver birch trees like a sleek black panther, the deep throaty roars of the engine making the fine hairs on Tillie's arm rise in a Mexican wave.

Blake's car was exactly like him. Potent. Powerful. Sexy.

Truffles decided the car was the perfect prey

and took off like a supersonic NASA rocket. Tillie lunged for her collar but missed and ended up falling onto her knees on the rough gravel. She clambered to her feet and inspected the bloody grazes to her knees. Why hadn't she worn jeans instead of a skirt? She picked out a couple of stones and, taking a tissue from inside her bra, dabbed at the blood.

Tillie limped to where Blake was standing next to his car. Truffles sat next to him as if she were the star pupil at obedience school.

Blake glanced at Tillie's knees and frowned. 'Are you okay?'

'No—thanks to you,' Tillie said. 'You could have called or texted to let me know you were coming. Truffles has a thing about cars. If I'd known you were going to visit I would've put her on the lead.'

'Let's get you inside to clean up those wounds. They look painful.' He offered her an arm but she sidestepped it and shot him a keep-away-from-me glare.

'I think you've helped me enough for one day,' Tillie said. 'Do you realise the whole village is abuzz with the news of our engagement? I've had to turn my phone off because the calls and texts haven't stopped with everyone's congratulations.'

His expression went from concerned to puzzled. Then his gaze zeroed in on the ring. 'But I thought you accepted my offer and—'

'Accept?' Tillie snorted. 'I did no such thing! I stupidly put your ring on to see what it looked like and it got stuck on my finger. Then I visited Mr Pendleton because the centre called to say he'd had a fall and he saw it there and laughed at me when I told him who gave it to me.'

'Laughed?'

Tillie clenched her teeth so hard she could have moonlighted as a nutcracker. 'Yes. Laughed. Apparently I'm too old-fashioned and sensible for someone like you and I have zero chance of ever taming you. But while Mr Pendleton didn't buy it, the nurse came in and thought it was the best news she'd ever heard and has since told everyone and now I'm engaged to you and the whole damn community is clapping their hands in raptures of joy because poor jilted Tillie Toppington has got herself a new man. I swear to God I'm so furious I could scream loud enough to blow out my voice box.'

Blake's mouth did that trying-not-to-smile thing. 'So why did you tell the old man I gave you the ring in the first place?'

Tillie rolled her eyes as if she were in a movie about an exorcist. 'Because the doctor told me Mr Pendleton was feeling a bit low and irritable after hitting his head so she said not to stress him too much. He saw the ring on my finger and asked me if my ex had come crawling back. I told him someone else had given it to me but he insisted I tell him who that someone was. Then I had to sit through three and a half hours of his paroxysms of laughter when I told him it was you.'

'How did you explain our relationship?'

Tillie loaded her voice with I've-got-you-now. 'I told him you came into the shop and fell in love with me at first sight.'

His laugh made something in her stomach tickle. 'Don't you mean love at first bite? One taste of your chocolate éclairs and I was hooked.'

Tillie was annoyed he found this so amusing. That he found *her* so amusing. She stabbed a finger at his chest. 'This whole flipping fiancée farce is all your fault.'

He captured her hand as if he was worried she would bore a hole right through his chest. Not that her finger could ever get through the layer of marble-hard muscle he had going on there. She'd need a jackhammer for that. His pecs were practically as big as the flagstones in McClelland Park's front hall.

'Did he say he was going to sell the Park to me?' he asked.

'Is that all you can think about?' Tillie pointed

at her own chest this time. 'This is *my* life we're talking about here. *My* reputation. What is everyone going to think?'

'They're going to think well done you for landing yourself a wealthy good-looking fiancé after that jerk screwed you over.'

'Yes, well, at least that's one thing he didn't get to do,' she said before she could filter her tongue.

A quick flash of concern crossed his features. 'What do you mean?'

'Never mind.' She turned to look at Truffles, who was now lying at Blake's feet like a devoted slave waiting to obey his master's next command. *Sickening. Just sickening.*

'Traitor,' she said to the dog. 'I knew Mr Pendleton should've chosen the whippet.'

Truffles showed the whites of her melting brown eyes and gave an I'm-way-too-cute-for-you-to-be-angry-at-me whine.

Blake chuckled. 'Cute mutt.' Then he looked at Tillie. 'Aren't you going to ask your new fiancé inside for a drink?'

'No. I am not.'

He gave a look not unlike the one Truffles had done moments earlier. 'Come on, Tillie. We have to get our history straight otherwise Jim Pendleton won't be the only one who's not going to buy our engagement.'

She speared him with a glare. 'I don't want people to buy it. I want this ridiculous situation to go away.'

'It's not going away until I get back this property,' he said. 'And, by the way, people are going to wonder why I'm not living here with you instead of at the B&B.'

'If you move in here that doesn't mean you get to make a move on me. *Comprende?*'

That dark twinkle was back in his gaze. 'We need to work on the old man to convince him to sell the Park to me now we're engaged.'

'I am *not* engaged to you.' Tillie spat the words out like lemon pips. 'Anyway, it's probably not legal to get an old man with memory problems to sign anything legally binding.'

Another flicker of concern passed over his features. 'Has he got dementia?'

'No, just a bit of temporary confusion from his fall,' she said. 'But I still don't think it would be right to take advantage of that.'

'No, of course not.' He gave an on-off smile. 'I'll just have to be patient, won't I?'

He didn't strike Tillie as a particularly patient man—not after 'proposing' to her within a couple of weeks of meeting her. But she couldn't help noticing the way he kept glancing at the house where he had spent the first ten years of his childhood. The ten-bedroom Georgian mansion was positioned on woodland-fringed acreage with a lake in front. There were both formal and wild gardens and a conservatory that made the most of the morning sun.

Tillie had moved in after Mr Pendleton's stroke two months ago to take care of Truffles and now hated the thought of ever leaving. She could well understand Blake's attachment to the place. If she had to picture a dream home then this wasn't far off it. Was it mean spirited of her to stop him staying here instead of the B&B? She had never had a permanent place to call home because her father's work as a vicar always required him to move into a vicarage owned by the parish. She had lived in the gamekeeper's cottage at Simon's parents' property for seven years, because when her father had been transferred she'd no longer been able to stay at the vicarage and had wanted to finish her final year at the local school and then go on to catering college. But she could imagine for someone whose family had lived in a place like McClelland Park for generation after generation, the emotional attachment would be so much greater.

Blake's gaze returned from surveying the house to the droplets of blood tracking a pathway down her shins. 'You really should get some antiseptic on those abrasions.'

Tillie had forgotten all about her knees. It was hard to concentrate on anything but the grey-blue of his eyes and the shape of his mouth when he spoke. She couldn't stop thinking about how his mouth would feel pressed to hers—whether it would be hard or soft or something in between. 'Yes, right, well, then…erm…would you like to come in and have a look around while you're here?' The invitation was out before she could stop it.

There was a spark of devilry in his gaze. 'Are you sure the old man won't mind an old-fashioned and sensible girl like you inviting a guy you only met a couple of weeks ago in?'

She held up her left hand, her expression wry. 'Why would he? We're engaged—remember?'

He grinned. 'How could I forget?'

CHAPTER THREE

BLAKE STEPPED OVER the threshold of his family's home and a wave of memories washed over him. For a moment—a brief moment—he had trouble controlling his composure. An ache spread from his heart to every corner and crevice of his chest—a tight, squeezing ache that snatched his breath away in degrees. Every room of this house contained memories—every window, every wall, every floorboard. He had spent the happiest years of his life here with the two people he'd loved more than anyone else in the world. This house epitomised for him that long-ago era of security and love and safety.

The colour scheme had been changed over the years and the furnishings, of course, but the overall structure was exactly the same. The mullioned windows that fed the light in from outside, the polished wooden floors that creaked now and again when you walked across them.

The staircase that led to the upper floors, the bannister he had slid down too many times to count. He could almost hear his mother's light cheery voice calling out to him as he came in the front door. He could almost hear the click-clack of her heels on the floorboards and the smell of her flowery perfume, the gentle weight of her arms as they gathered him close in a loving hug…

'I'll leave you to have a wander around,' Tillie said. 'I'm going to clean up my knees.'

Blake was pulled out of his reverie. 'Let me help you. Besides, it was my fault you hurt yourself.'

'I can put on my own plasters.' Her voice had a note of icy hauteur he found amusing. But then a lot about her was amusing. Amusing and refreshing and tempting.

'I insist.'

She let out a *whatever* sigh and turned in the direction of the nearest bathroom. He couldn't tear his eyes away from her pert behind, the way her skirt swished from side to side over it as she walked.

He wondered if he could persuade her to let him stay with her here. He was reasonably comfortable at the B&B, if you could call comfortable a bed you disappeared into like a cloud—all except for his ankles and feet, that was. He almost gave himself concussion every time he walked through the door and Mrs Rosethorne and her all-you-can-eat breakfasts were doing their best to undo all the work he'd put in with his personal trainer.

What was Tillie's main issue? It was a big house. There were enough rooms for them to avoid contact if she preferred not to interact with him. Although, the sort of interaction he had in mind required close contact. Skin-to-skin contact.

Blake followed her into the bathroom and crouched down in front of her.

'What are you doing?' she said, wide-eyed.

He placed a gentle hand on her leg just above her knee. 'Inspecting the wounds.'

'Get your hands off me.' Her voice had that starchy schoolmistress-tone thing going on.

He glanced up at her. 'You've got a piece of gravel in your knee. Hand me some tweezers and I'll get it out for you.'

Indecision flittered across her features. Then she let out another sigh and rummaged in the cupboard near the basin and handed him a pair of tweezers, some antiseptic and some cotton pads. 'Go for it,' she said, sitting on the closed toilet seat. 'I never was one for playing doctors and nurses.'

Blake smiled and set to work. 'Am I hurting you?'

'A bit.'

'Sorry.'

Within a short time he had the grazes cleansed and covered with plasters and then got to his feet. Tillie rose from the toilet seat with twin pools of colour in her cheeks.

Damn, he loved to see a woman who could still blush.

'Thank you,' she said, avoiding his gaze.

'My pleasure.' He put his hand underneath her chin and raised her eyes to his. 'You have great legs, by the way.'

The colour in her face deepened three shades. 'Look, Mr McClelland, I—'

'That's a bit formal for an engaged couple, don't you think?'

Her brown eyes simmered like overheated caramel. Her gaze slipped to his mouth and she drew in a jagged breath and the tip of her tongue darted out and left a layer of moisture over her lips. 'B-Blake, then,' she said in a voice as raspy as the emery board sitting on the bathroom counter.

Blake slid a hand along the side of her face to splay his fingers underneath her cloud of springy chestnut hair that smelt of sweet peas. He felt her shudder as if his touch had set off an involuntary tremor in her body. She was so close he could feel her hips brushing against his, stirring his blood into doing push ups. Could she feel what she was doing to him? He looked between each of her eyes in a back and forth motion, watching as her pupils flared like spilled ink.

She could.

Tillie's hands came up to lie flat on his chest, her luscious breasts pressing against him until it was all he could do not to bury his face in the cleavage hidden behind her conservative cotton blouse. He wanted to kiss her. Badly. But he wanted it to be her idea, not something she could accuse him of setting up.

He put his hands on her upper arms and gently put her from him. 'So, here's what I think we should tell people. We met a while back and recently fell madly in love.'

She gave him the sort of look a hardened sceptic gave a faith healer. 'Met where?'

'Where everyone meets these days—online.'

'I don't meet people like that,' she said. 'I prefer the old-fashioned way of actually seeing a person in the flesh first.'

Blake began to undo his top buttons of his shirt.

Her eyes rounded until her eyebrows almost met her hairline. 'What are you doing?'

'Allowing you to meet me in the flesh.'

She whipped around and stalked out of the bathroom. 'You're unbelievable. You think you're so damn irresistible, don't you?' She turned back around to flash him a glare as hot as a flame. 'Well, guess what, Blake McClelland? This is one scalp you won't be able to add to your well-worn bedpost.' She pointed her finger towards the front door. 'Now get out before I set the dog on you.'

Blake glanced at Truffles, who was lying on the floor chewing on a ballet flat that was looking more like a dead animal than a shoe. The dog stopped chewing and wagged its tail back and forth along the floor like a fluffy broom and gave a soft little whine.

Blake looked back at Tillie. 'Look, I'm fine with us not sleeping together during our engagement. It's not a mandatory part of the deal. But I still think I should stay here for the sake of appearances.'

There was a small silence.

'Why isn't it?' she asked, cheeks darkening again. 'Don't you…fancy me?'

He fancied her *too* damn much. He couldn't think of the last time he'd felt so turned on by a woman. Maybe it was because she was resisting him. Dating had become a little too easy over the years. It didn't take much of an effort to get a woman into his bed. Was that why he was feeling a bit bored by it all just lately? The dinner-drink-bed combo was foolproof but predictable. This whiff of a new challenge made his blood tick and his pulse race. Or maybe it wasn't so much the challenge, but the fact it was Tillie.

'Come back over here and I'll prove it,' he said.

She pressed her lips together until they were white. 'You're laughing at me. I know you are.' She turned her back and hugged her arms around her middle. 'Please leave.'

Blake came back over to her and stood behind her with his hands resting on the tops of her shoulders. She flinched like a flighty filly as if torn between wanting to be stroked and wanting to flee. 'Hey,' he said.

She dipped out from under his hold and cast him a look that would have stripped three centuries of paintwork off the walls. 'I want out of this engagement before I'm made a laughing stock. Again.'

'Declaring bankruptcy would be worse.'

Uncertainty passed over her features and her teeth sank into her lower lip. But then a defiant spark came back in her gaze. 'I'll sell your ring and pay off my debts that way.'

'You could,' Blake said, with a slow smile. 'But you'd have to get it off your finger first.'

Her anger was so palpable he could feel it

crackling in the air like static. Her eyes blazed and her fists clenched and her body vibrated. She whooshed out a breath. 'It seems I haven't got much choice but to go along with this. Too many people already think we're engaged and I'll look an idiot if I retract what I've said so far. If you pay off my debts I'll agree to this stupid charade, but there have to be some ground rules laid down first.'

Blake wondered what had finally swayed her. Was it just the money she owed? It was certainly an amount that would be enough for the average person to lose a little sleep over. Was it about losing face in the village? Or was it because of her affection for old Mr Pendleton—she didn't want to upset him so was prepared to run with the charade? Or did she plan to resist Blake to prove a point? Who did she want to prove it to? To him or herself?

'Scan and email the bills to me and I'll sort them out this evening,' he said. 'And as to rules— the only one I insist on is whenever we're out in public you behave like a woman in love.'

Her eyes fired off another round of sparks. 'And what about when we're alone?'

'I'll leave that to you to decide.'

Her chin jerked up. 'I've already decided. I wouldn't sleep with you if you paid me.'

'I'm not in the habit of paying for sex,' Blake said.

Her teeth started to tug at her lower lip as if the mere thought of the money she owed was enough to send her into a spiralling panic bad enough to invite an axe murderer to move in as long as he settled her debt. She released her lip and returned her gaze to his. 'You can move in tomorrow once I've had time to prepare a room. But you need to know, I'm not usually the sort of girl to live with someone I've only just met.'

'Did you live with your ex?'

'No…not really.'

Blake frowned. 'What does that mean?'

'I rented a cottage at Simon's parents' estate but he didn't share it with me,' she said. 'His parents were a bit old-fashioned about that sort of thing.'

Why couldn't they have let it to her for free? Local gossip informed him Simon's parents weren't as wealthy as he was, but neither were they sitting on street corners with a tin cup in their hand. 'You *rented* it?' he said.

'Yes.' Her jaw clenched and her eyes flashed as if the memory annoyed her. 'And they didn't give me back the bond after I moved out. His mother said I scratched her precious walnut coffee table but I did no such thing. Not that I didn't wish I had afterwards. I wanted to take a pickaxe to the whole damn cottage until there was nothing left but kindling.'

Blake suppressed a smile. Tillie might have a reputation as a mild-mannered angel but it didn't take much to scratch that Goody Two-Shoes façade to find a passionate and feisty little virago inside. 'Sounds like you had a lucky escape. Once I move in tomorrow, I'll take you out to dinner. It'll be a way to let the locals know we're the real deal.'

Her brown eyes narrowed. 'Just dinner, right?'

'Just dinner.'

Once Blake had left, Tillie stalked back into the sitting room and let out a curse word. Three curse words. Words she had never said before. Words that would have made her God-fearing father have a conniption if he'd heard her.

Blake McClelland was the most infuriating man she'd ever met—infuriating and way too charming and attractive. She had been so close to making a fool of herself—acting like a gauche schoolgirl mooning over his mouth as if she was gagging for him to kiss her. She had been just about gagging, but that was beside the point.

Truffles came into the sitting room and jumped on the sofa to look out of the window as if checking to see where Blake had gone and started whining piteously.

'Oh, for pity's sake,' Tillie said to the dog. 'Did you have to make such a fool of yourself with him? You're supposed to be on my side.'

Truffles gave a doggy sigh and flopped down on the sofa, resting her muzzle on her paws and giving another my-world-is-over whine.

Tillie flicked her eyelids in disdain. 'You might think he's the best thing since those dog treats I baked for you, but I know what he's up to. He thinks he can hook me like he hooks all his other lovers. Well, he's in for a big surprise because he could crook that little finger of his all he likes. Unlike you, I *can* resist him.'

She had the willpower. She had the discipline. She had the self-control.

He thought he could toy with her to fill in the time until he secured his deal over the property. She was going to give that overblown confidence of his a wake-up call. If he thought he could stride into town and pick her up like a cake off the counter then he was in for a big disappointment. He could take her out to a hundred dinners—a thousand. He could move into the house but she was *not* going to sleep with him.

But she would make everyone think she was.

Tillie was determined to show everyone in

the village she had the ability to attract a full-blooded man. Even Mr Pendleton would be convinced once she executed her plan. No one would call her old-fashioned and too conservative once she had been seen out and about with Blake McClelland. Her Goody Two-Shoes reputation was in for a rapid makeover.

She would continue to hate him behind closed doors. Hate and dislike and loathe him. A pity about the issue of her physical attraction to him, but still—she couldn't win them all. He could pay her debts and she wouldn't suffer a flicker of conscience about him doing so. If he wanted her to act like a woman in love in public then that was what she would do—with bells and whistles and hearts and flowers.

Tillie turned back to the dog and smiled a witch-stirring-a-cauldron smile. 'I'm going to lay it on so thick and so cloyingly sweet he won't know what hit him.'

Blake visited Mr Pendleton the following day with a gift of a new bestseller and a small bottle of Scotch. The old man narrowed his eyes when Blake came in. 'I wondered when you were going to show up again. What's this I hear about you giving Tillie an engagement ring? You think I'm so stupid not to see what you're doing?'

Blake sat in the chair beside the bed and crossed one ankle over his thigh. 'And here I was thinking you were a romantic. Didn't you tell me you fell in love with your wife within minutes of meeting her?'

Mr Pendleton's features softened a fraction at the mention of his wife. 'Yes, well, they don't make women like my Velma these days... Mind you, Tillie comes close.' His expression sharpened again and his eyes bored into Blake's. 'She's a good girl. Too good for the likes of you.'

Blake couldn't help feeling a spike of irritation. Admittedly he had a bit of a reputation as a playboy, but neither was he out there robbing banks or ripping off little old ladies. 'Surely Tillie should be the judge of that, not you or the rest of the village.'

The old man shook his head. 'Thing is... I'm not sure Tillie knows what she wants. She saved up for years for that wedding. The dress alone cost a fortune and I have it on good authority she only chose the design because Simon's mother pressured her. I offered to help her with the money she owes but she won't take it off me.'

'I've sorted out all that for her,' Blake said. 'You don't have to worry about it any more.'

Mr Pendleton's gaze still contained a glittering sheen of you-can't-fool-me cynicism. 'Have you moved in with her yet?'

'I'm heading over there tonight. Thanks for giving the okay about it, by the way.'

'You must be more charming than I thought. Have you set a wedding date?'

'We're still getting used to being a couple,' Blake said. 'I don't want to rush her after her last relationship.'

Mr Pendleton made a *phhfft* noise. 'Call *that* a relationship? That boy didn't even sleep with her. She's as untouched as a nun.' He gave Blake another probing look. 'I bet a man like you wouldn't settle for a peck on the cheek and a bit of tame handholding. That's how I knew he wasn't right for her. I know he's a man of faith and all that, but chemistry is chemistry. You either have it as a couple or you don't.'

Blake was doing his level best to disguise his shock.

Tillie was a virgin?

How had she got to her mid-twenties without having sex? He'd heard via Mrs Rosethorne at the B&B Tillie had been engaged to her fiancé for three years and dated him since she was sixteen. Surely her fiancé would have pushed for more? Even a man of faith had hormones, didn't he? Was that why she reacted to Blake the way she did? With that hungry look in her eyes, as if someone was offering her something she had longed denied herself?

Wait a minute.

Blake wished his conscience hadn't shown up for duty. How could he have a fling with her if she was a virgin? He didn't do virgins. Virgins were rosy-cheeked princesses waiting for princes to show up on a white horse. Virgins wanted the whole package: marriage and babies and a white picket fence.

He wasn't signing up for any of that.

Not one bit of it.

Mr Pendleton gave Blake the squinty eye. 'Everything all right? You want me to call the nurse? You're looking a little pale.'

Blake forced a smile and got to his feet. 'I have to get going. Call me if you change your mind about the Park.'

Mr Pendleton snorted. 'Tillie might fall for your charm but I'm not so much of a pushover. I'll sell when I'm good and ready and not a moment before.'

Blake stalled by the end of the old man's bed. 'Will you at least give me your word you won't sell it to anyone else?'

The old man's gaze was unwavering. 'Will

you give me your word you won't break Tillie's heart?'

Blake tried not to flinch under the old man's piercing scrutiny. 'You never know—she might be the one to break mine.'

Mr Pendleton gave a mercurial smile. 'I hope so.'

CHAPTER FOUR

TILLIE WAS IN the shop serving one of her regulars when Blake came in that afternoon. She had so far survived Mrs Jeffries's questions about how she had met Blake and how he'd proposed—with a good bit of embellishment, of course.

She handed Mrs Jeffries her date and ginger scones over the counter. 'Ah, here he is now.' Tillie sent Blake a dazzling smile and gave him a little finger wave. 'Hello, sweetie pie. I was just telling Mrs Jeffries how romantic your proposal was. How you got down on bended knee and begged for me to say yes. I told her you had a little cry when I did. Well, not just a *little* cry.' She looked at Mrs Jeffries again. 'He was bawling his eyes out. I was about to call for sand bags to stop him flooding the joint. I've never seen a man so in touch with his emotions. Wasn't that awfully sweet?'

Mrs Jeffries made oohing and aahing sounds. 'Everyone's so happy for you, Tillie.'

Blake was a terrifyingly good actor, for he simply smiled. Tillie knew he wouldn't let her get away with it for too long, but, in a way, that was part of the thrill of doing it. She *wanted* to spar with him. Their verbal exchanges excited her in a way no one else's conversation had before. She saw the I'll-get-you-for-that-later glint in his grey-blue eyes and a shiver coursed down her spine like the tickle of a strip of tinsel paper.

'Aren't you going to kiss me hello, babe?' he said. 'I'm sure Mrs Jeffries won't mind.'

'Of course not,' Mrs Jeffries said, smiling indulgently.

Tillie came from behind the counter. What harm was there in a chaste brush of the lips? Actors did it all the time and much more than that, too. She came to stand in front of him and planted her hands on his chest and looked into his wickedly glinting eyes.

Better get it over with.

She closed her eyes halfway and lifted her mouth to his descending one.

The first brush of his mouth against hers sent a frisson of heat right through to her core. The second brush wasn't a brush—it was a lingering pressure that made her lips open on a gasp and allow his tongue to glide in with such toe-curling expertise every cell in her body jerked upright as if jolted awake from a long sleep. His tongue grazed hers, calling it into a sexy duel that made her knees feel as if someone had taken her bones out. She leaned into his embrace, another cascading shiver going down her spine when his strongly muscled arms gathered her closer. His hands moved from the small of her back to cup her rear, bringing her flush against him. She could feel the growing ridge of his erection, thick and urgent, speaking to her feminine form with such primal power it was almost shocking.

How could she be responding to him like this? She didn't even like him and yet her body craved his as an addict did a forbidden drug.

Tillie wasn't sure who broke the kiss but she had a sneaking suspicion it might have been him. She lowered herself off her tippy toes and smiled. 'Well, nice to know you're pleased to see me.'

Blake's smile told her he wasn't finished with her yet. 'Always, babe. Always.'

Mrs Jeffries left the shop just as Joanne came in from her lunch break. Joanne's face broke into a wide smile. 'Hi, Blake. Congratulations, by the way. Best news ever.'

'Thanks,' he said. 'I think so too. I've called

in to take Tillie out for a drive. Can you hold the fort for half an hour?'

'But I've got to—' Tillie began.

'Sure, no problem,' Joanne said. 'Tillie was about to have a break anyway. Have fun!'

When they stepped outside, Blake held out his hand and Tillie had no choice but to slip hers into it because there were villagers about doing their errands at the various shops along her section of the street. His hand was warm and dry and almost swallowed hers whole. There was a faintly erotic undercurrent in the way he held her hand. His thumb was absently—it might not have been absently but deliberately—stroking the flesh until every nerve was tinglingly aware of each back and forth movement of his thumb-pad. She was annoyed with herself for being so damn responsive to his touch. Surely there was something wrong with her? It wasn't normal to be so…so…*sensually aware*…was it?

Tillie walked with him to where his car was parked a couple of spaces down from her shop. 'Where are we going?'

'A drive.'

'Where to?'

'Just a drive.'

She frowned at him once he'd taken his place behind the wheel after settling her in the passenger side. She couldn't read his expression for it seemed a shutter had come down now they no longer had an audience. She turned back to face the front and didn't speak again until they were clear of the village and out on the country lane that led past McClelland Park. 'I do have a job to do, you know. I run a small business that requires me to be there eight to ten hours a—'

'Why didn't you tell me you were a virgin?'

Tillie blinked in shock. How on earth did he know that? Who else knew? It wasn't something she talked about with any of her friends. Although, come to think of it, a few months ago Simon had been prone to lecturing anyone who would listen about the benefits of being celibate. She wondered now if he'd done that because he'd been sleeping with his new girlfriend at the time. Or was it because everyone in the village saw Tillie as conservative and old-fashioned? A nineteenth-century throwback too prudish to show an ankle in public. Maybe they secretly blamed her for Simon running off with someone else. 'I can't imagine how you came by that information or how you could possibly believe it's true.'

'Is it?'

Tillie folded her arms across her chest and stared straight ahead. 'I'm not going to answer such an impertinent question.'

The car slowed to a stop by the side of the road and Blake turned off the engine and swivelled in his seat to look at her. 'So it *is* true.'

She chanced a glance to find him watching her with a thoughtful expression. 'So what if it is?'

'How old are you?'

'Twenty-four.'

'A bit old to be a virgin in this day and age, isn't it?'

Tillie looked at the cows snatching mouthfuls of lush green grass in the field nearby. It was a bit old, but she'd only agreed to it because Simon had insisted. She hadn't questioned it because she knew her parents, and then her stepmother too, had also abstained before marriage. It was common with people of faith; there were even celibacy movements amongst young people all around the globe. But she couldn't help wondering if Simon had never truly wanted her but had been using her as a back-up plan until someone more attractive came along. The absence of a strong pull of attraction in her relationship with Simon was only apparent to her now she had met Blake. No amount of mountain-shifting faith, no strength of conviction could withstand the incendiary heat that flared between her and Blake.

'Simon didn't believe in sex before marriage,'

she said. 'Not unless it was with a size zero blonde who looked like she should still be in school.'

'You didn't…try and change his mind?' Blake asked after a small silence.

Tillie had tried that once and it had spectacularly failed. She still cringed in embarrassment thinking about it. Simon had gone all preachy on her and made her feel abnormal for giving in to 'base desires', as he'd called them.

'You mean seduce him?' She gave a snorting laugh. 'Not my forte at all, I'm afraid.'

'I don't know about that.'

She couldn't stop her gaze going to the curve of his mouth. She swallowed and dragged her eyes back to his. 'Can we talk about something else?'

He reached out a hand and picked up a loose curl and slowly but surely wound it around one of his fingers. 'You're a beautiful woman. Don't let anyone tell you you're not.'

Tillie leaned closer as if to inspect the function of his eyes. 'Do you need glasses? Because I'm not sure what school of beauty you subscribe to but no way would I ever describe myself as beautiful. Passable maybe, but not beautiful.'

He still had hold of her hair, inexorably drawing her closer and closer as if reeling her into his orbit. His gaze kept going to her mouth as if, like her, he couldn't stop himself. 'You're too hard on yourself. I find intelligence enormously attractive. Sexy too.'

So did Tillie. But then, she found everything about Blake McClelland attractive and sexy. 'Right, well, thanks for the compliment but I have a business to run so if you're done with talking then—'

'When I asked you to play this charade with me I intended to sleep with you,' Blake said, releasing her hair to sit back against his seat.

Tillie gave him a pointed look. 'Was my consent a part of your plan?'

A frown snapped his brows together. 'Of course it was. I'm not the sort of man who forces himself on a woman.' He let out a gust of a breath and the frown relaxed but only slightly. 'I'm also not the sort of man who gets involved with virgins.'

All virgins? Or only plus-size ones who aren't considered classically beautiful?

'So what's with the anti-virgin bias?' she asked.

'Women who've waited to have sex until they meet the right person are usually waiting for the fairy tale,' he said. 'It wouldn't be fair to sleep with them and then ride off into the sunset without them.'

'You don't see yourself getting married one day?'

'No.'

'Better not tell the rest of the village that or they'll be after you with feathers and a pot of tar,' Tillie said.

He gave a soft laugh that didn't sound all that amused. 'Yes, well, you think I don't know that? Which is why we're not going to get down to business.'

She arched her brow. 'Did I say I was going to sleep with you?'

The look he gave her made her want to tear off her clothes and throw herself at him then and there. 'I haven't had anyone turn me down before.'

Tillie felt a faint thrill at being the first. Faint because she didn't want to turn him down. She wanted to crush her mouth to his and open her lips for the smooth thrust of his tongue, to push her breasts up against his chest, to push her hips against his and feel the stirring of his arousal in the throb of his blood.

She wanted. She wanted. She wanted.

The air seemed to pulsate with the sexual energy that flared between their locked gazes.

'Don't even think about it.' His voice had a note of stern authority.

'You don't know what I'm thinking,' Tillie said, quickly schooling her features.

One corner of his mouth came up. 'Don't I?' He reached out a fingertip and traced the line of her mouth like someone reading Braille—the top lip and the lower one, as if memorising their contours.

Tillie hadn't known how many nerve endings were in her lips. She hadn't known how hard it would be to resist such a caress. She hadn't known she didn't have the willpower to. *Where was her willpower?* 'Tell me what I'm thinking, then.'

His finger grazed the curve of her cheek. 'You're thinking how it would be—you and me—getting it on.'

'Actually, I'm thinking of the christening cake I have to decorate before the weekend,' Tillie said.

'Liar.'

His fingertip found her ear and did a slow circuit of her cartilage until she had to hold her breath to stop from whimpering in delight. His mouth came closer as if in slow motion, his warm hint-of-cinnamon-scented breath mingling with hers in the tiny space that separated their mouths. She closed the distance and touched her mouth against his with a feather-light brush, but it wasn't enough. She wanted more. She pushed her lips against his in a playful nudge, a part of her looking from above and wondering where she had been hiding this sensual side of herself for all these years.

Blake took control of the kiss with a muttered groan, his arms gathering her closer, almost crushing her as his mouth moved with passionate urgency against hers. She opened to the commanding thrust of his tongue, welcoming it into the cavern of her mouth, tangling with it in a cat and mouse caper that made the desire deep in her core break free from its restraints. It flooded her body like a sizzling hot tide, sweeping away all the reasons why she shouldn't be encouraging this sort of interaction with him. Right now all she could think about was how amazing his mouth felt on hers. How thrilling it was to have him as turned on by her as she was by him. The guttural sounds he was making made her shiver all over as if someone had dusted her body with sparkly glitter and filled her blood with bubbles.

No one had ever kissed her like this. Not with such heat and intensity. Not with such ferocious desire that matched her own. She could feel her body preparing itself—her female flesh aching for friction to bring the release it craved.

She could hear the noises she was making. Primal noises. Noises of encouragement and approval. Noises of pleasure—whimpers and gasps and little groans that sounded nothing like her. She linked her arms around his neck, pushing her breasts as close to him as the gear console allowed, her fingers toying with the wavy ends of his dark brown hair that were brushing against his collar. She breathed in the clean male scent of him, the notes of lime and citrus, tasted the hint of mint on his tongue, ached for him with a pulse throbbing like a drum beat between her thighs. Desire hijacked her body, making it a slave to the sensations powering through her body—shockingly addictive sensations his touch evoked. Every movement of his mouth, every thrust and glide of his tongue, every nip and nudge of his teeth stirred her senses into a fireball of longing, sending arrows of heat to her core.

Blake suddenly pulled away, breathing heavily. 'Okay. Time out.' He sat back against his driver's seat and took a steadying breath, his hands gripping the steering wheel as if to anchor himself.

Tillie sat back and smoothed her hands down her skirt, trying to get her body to settle down but it wasn't listening. Needs she hadn't been aware of were thrumming inside her—deep, deep inside her. If she squeezed her legs together it only made it worse. It was a shock to realise how close she'd been to begging him to finish what he'd started.

Or had he started it?

There was a painfully long silence.

'Aren't you going to say anything?' she asked.

He opened and closed his fingers on the steering wheel for a moment, his brows still jammed together over his eyes. 'I'm not sure it's a good idea for me to move in to the Park straight away.'

Not a good idea? It was a brilliant idea. No one would think she was too old-fashioned once she had Blake installed at the house. 'But you have to. I've told everyone you're moving in tonight.' She gave him a probing look. 'You *do* want McClelland Park back, right?'

'You know I do. But I have some business to see to in Edinburgh for a few days.'

'You didn't mention anything about business yesterday when you came to see me at the house. We were going to go for dinner.'

His face got a boxed-up look about it. 'It's come up since then. It's…urgent.'

What was urgent? His business or his need to get away from temptation? It was weird thinking of herself as a temptation. She had never tempted Simon beyond his control. Not once in eight years. A thrill trickled through her body at the thought of Blake wanting her so badly he felt the need to distance himself.

Maybe size zero blondes didn't have all the fun after all.

He turned over the engine. 'I'd better get you back to work.' And glancing over his shoulder, he drove back out into the lane, spraying arcs of loose gravel out from under the spinning tyres.

Okay, so that went well.

Blake drove away after dropping Tillie back at her shop. He couldn't get that kiss out of his mind. He'd been like a horny teenager necking by the side of the road. He was supposed to be putting the brakes on now he'd found out she was a virgin. But as soon as her lips met his it was all he could do to keep his hands off her. Her inexperience was supposed to be helping him keep his distance, but instead it was drawing him to her like an alcoholic to a free wine tasting.

Her mouth was so soft and sexy beneath his. It responded to his as if he were feeding her the air she needed to stay alive. It had damn near killed him to pull back. He'd wanted to keep on kissing her, to touch her, to peel those clothes off her and put his mouth on those gorgeous breasts he'd felt crushed up against his chest.

He had to get control of himself. He was supposed to be focussed on getting McClelland Park back, not having a fling with a girl who had been saving herself for Prince Charming. Tillie responded to him as if she had never been kissed properly before. But then, maybe she hadn't if her ex had had his interest invested elsewhere. She kissed with her whole body, throwing so much passion into the mix he could only imagine what it would be like to make love to her.

You could offer her a fling.

The thought nibbled at the edges of his conscience like a mouse at wainscoting. Tillie was attracted to him; there was no doubt in his mind about that. But would she agree to a short-term fling when she had the fairy tale as her ultimate goal? Girls like Tillie did not do flings. Girls like Tillie waited years for the right guy to put a ring on their finger and promise them for ever.

Blake was a for-now guy. He had a mission and once it was completed he would be moving on. And he wasn't taking anyone with him when he left. No baggage meant exactly that: No. Baggage. He travelled light when it came to his emotions because that was the way to keep control. Control was his thing. He didn't need to sit on some therapist's sofa to know it had something to do with losing his mother when he was a kid. He'd seen what happened when emotions took over. They stopped people thinking clearly. They confused and distorted things.

He kept his head clear by focussing on the task. So what if he was a workaholic? It was his determined focus that had clawed back the wealth—and more—that had been lost when his father had his breakdown. Blake's ability to make tough business decisions without involving emotion had been the blueprint for his success. As soon as people allowed feelings into the mix things started to get messy. He had seen previously successful companies fall over as soon as feelings started flirting with the numbers. It was numbers you could rely on, not spur-of-the-moment impulses.

He'd thought it would be so simple talking Tillie into helping him to get McClelland Park back. When he'd heard on the village grapevine about her being jilted and the debt she was in, he'd thought he could use her situation to his advantage: a month pretending to be his fiancée in exchange for clearing her debts. Too easy…or so he'd thought. But he hadn't considered the aftermath of such an arrangement. He planned to have his father live at the Park in the not too distant future. If Blake messed with Tillie the whole darn village would run him out of town and perhaps make things awkward for his dad. She was the village saint and he would be asking to have his kneecaps taken out with a cricket bat if he did the wrong thing by her.

Although she wasn't averse to messing with him, the cheeky little minx. The way she'd laid it on with a trowel in front of her customer with all that rubbish about him weeping over his proposal. He had nothing against men crying, but it had been a long time since his tear ducts had had a workout.

But that was what he liked about Tillic. She wasn't a pushover. She gave as good as she got and didn't seem in the least fazed by being out-matched by her opponent. He was looking for-ward to further interactions with her, even if it meant he'd have to shackle and double padlock his desire.

Anyway, a bout of celibacy might do him good. *Really looking forward to that.*

Not.

CHAPTER FIVE

TILLIE HAD TAKEN Truffles to see Mr Pendleton and was back at McClelland Park keeping an eye on some cookies she had baking in the oven. She hadn't seen Blake for almost a week. When he'd first told her he was going to be away she'd been worried about what people would think given she'd announced to everyone he was moving in with her. But as each day passed with little or no contact from him, she felt strangely deflated, like a solitary balloon left behind after a party. She didn't want to admit how much she was looking forward to seeing him. Nor did she want to admit how boring her life was without him coming into the shop and giving her those glinting looks across the counter. She couldn't even look at a chocolate éclair now without a frisson passing over her flesh.

Tillie sent a text to Blake saying she'd leave a

key to McClelland Park under a loose flagstone near the front door for when he got back in case she was still at work.

Mr Pendleton was still refusing to believe she was really engaged to Blake. And it certainly hadn't helped when he'd heard Blake was in Scotland. But because of his memory issues, the staff at the respite centre reassured her it was just a phase and he would hopefully come out of it soon.

Every person who came into the shop stopped to chat about how wonderful it was she had found true love at last. Tillie was so good at lying now even *she* was starting to believe she was actually in love with Blake. The flutters in her tummy every time his name was mentioned made her wonder if her mind and her body were playing tricks on her. Surely you couldn't *act* your way into feeling something?

Tillie couldn't decide whether to be embarrassed everyone thought she was 'doing it' with Blake or disappointed she was not. Ever since those kisses her body had been feeling restless. It was as if a hunger had been awakened and nothing but him would satisfy it. If she closed her eyes she could recall every second of his mouth on hers, the way it felt, the way it tasted, the way his stubble left graze marks on her skin that she had to use make-up to cover.

When he'd first come to her with his plan, his intention had clearly been to seduce her into the bargain. But since finding out she was a virgin he had pulled back…apart from that kiss, that was. Could she indulge in a little fling with him? It wasn't as if she was going to fall in love with him. Her mind could play all the tricks it liked on her. She wasn't going to fall in love with anyone. No, siree. Not after the last time. Blake would be a means to an end just as he'd intended her to be for him.

What was the point of abstaining from sex when she had no intention of ever marrying? Not now. Not after being publicly humiliated at the wedding she had planned and looked forward to with such hope for the future. That was why she kept her wedding cake and dress as a reminder of her foolishness. A reminder of how stupid she had been to believe in the fairy tale.

The fairy tale sucked.

It was a big fat double-crossing lie.

It was a trap for romantic fools who thought life wasn't fulfilling without a partner. She could do just fine without one. Coupledom wasn't for her any more. No more pandering to a man. No more cooking meals she didn't like just because he liked them. No more watching bloodthirsty action movies or tediously boring sporting matches.

Single and Loving It. That would be her... *eventually*.

The engagement ring was still on Tillie's finger so she figured she might as well make the most of it. She suspected she would have to go on a crash diet for a month to get it off. No amount of hand cream or soap or butter would make it budge. She had to put on sterile gloves when she worked with pastry or cookie dough because she didn't want to get it dirty. But once the month was up that ring would be cut off and her ties with Blake cut, too.

But not before she had a bit of fun first.

Tillie took out the first batch of peanut butter cookies and slid in the next tray of chocolate chip. Truffles pricked up her ears, gave a bark and bolted out of the kitchen and started to scratch at the front door to be let out. Tillie pulled off her plastic gloves, wiped her hands on her apron and went to open the door to see Blake's black sports car coming to a stop in front of the fountain on the circular driveway in front of the house. He unfolded himself from behind the wheel with the sort of athletic grace she could only envy. When she exited a car, she looked like a baby elephant trying to squeeze through a cat flap.

Blake was carrying a bunch of pearly pink roses, not quite white but not fully pink, either.

He handed them to her with a crooked smile. 'Thought you might like these.'

Tillie buried her face in the fragrant blooms, suddenly embarrassed at the thought of him moving in with her. Had she done the wrong thing agreeing to it? What if it got…awkward? She had never lived with anyone other than her father and stepmother. What if Blake didn't take up her offer of a fling? The house might be big, but it wouldn't be big enough for her to avoid him then. 'They're gorgeous. I love the colour.'

'That pink reminds me of your cheeks when I make you blush.'

She could feel her cheeks doing exactly that. No one could make her blush more than him. He only had to look at her with those twinkling grey-blue eyes and her face would be aflame. Had he thought about the kisses they'd shared? Had he relived every second of them or had he occupied himself with someone else?

The thought was jarring. Like finding a fly in the cookie dough. There was nothing to stop him carrying on with his freewheeling playboy lifestyle. Their 'engagement' was a charade. No one had made any promises.

But if he was going to sleep with someone, why couldn't it be her?

The more Tillie thought about it, the more

sensible and convenient it seemed. It would be a chance for her to finally get her V plates off. She could indulge in a hot, no-strings fling with him as a way to celebrate rather than bemoan her single status. That was what singletons did, wasn't it? Had heaps of fun sex without the pressure of a relationship with expectations and responsibilities.

'So, how was your trip up north?' Tillie asked.

'Boring, actually.'

'So, they don't have burlesque dancers in Scotland?' The smile she gave him would have made a fox envious.

Blake sent her a mock glower but she could see his eyes were smiling. 'That was a stitch up by a mate of mine—a drunk mate of mine. He thought it'd be funny to have some scantily clad dancers hang out in my room while we were at an investment conference in Vegas. The press made a big thing of it, of course.'

His explanation pleased her in a way she couldn't quite explain. Or maybe it was because she was secretly glad he wasn't the sort of man to have sordid parties with Vegas showgirls.

'Would you like some dinner?' Tillie asked after a slight pause. 'I've got enough for two. Actually, I always have enough for two. I'm still learning how to cook for one person.'

'Sure, if it's no trouble? We could go out if you'd prefer.'

Tillie flashed her best wry smile. 'Cooking is my thing. It's the one thing I'm good at.'

'I'm sure you're good at lots of things.' Blake's gaze went to her mouth for a nanosecond. 'Not just good—excellent.'

'I'm…erm…just going to put these in some water,' she said. 'Why don't you make yourself at home? Sorry, that must sound weird, someone telling you to make yourself at home in what used to be your home. I've given you one of the larger spare rooms. I haven't moved Mr Pendleton's things out of the master suite because, well, it didn't seem the right thing to do just yet.'

'That's fine, I wasn't expecting to move in there yet.' He sniffed the air. 'The house looks and smells the same, too. What are you making?'

'Cookies. I do a lot of my baking for the shop here as it keeps the workspace clear for my decorating.'

Tillie was expecting him to go get his bags from the car and head upstairs to settle in, but instead he followed her into the kitchen. He pulled out and sat on one of the chairs at the large scrubbed pine table in the centre of the room, crossing one ankle over his knee, his gaze moving about the room as if recalling the times when he'd sat there as a child. She wondered if coming back here was difficult for him, stirring memories of his childhood and the loss he'd suffered.

Tillie sorted out the flowers but became conscious of his gaze resting on her. She glanced up from the roses and gave him a lopsided smile. 'You can have one if you like. You're not allergic to peanuts, are you?'

'No.' He took one of the peanut butter cookies off the cooling rack and bit into it and chewed, making *mmm, it's good* noises as he did so.

The oven timer sounded and she snatched up her oven mitts and bent down to take out the next tray.

'My mother used to bake,' Blake said into the silence. 'She used to let me help her.'

Tillie put the cookies on the cooling rack and looked at him. 'You must have been devastated when she died.'

He didn't speak for a moment, but stared at the half-eaten cookie he was holding as if wondering how it got there.

'It hit my father hard,' he finally said. 'His work suffered. Lost heaps of money in bad business decisions. Got exploited by people who should have been helping him, not ripping him off.'

Tillie couldn't believe how tragic it all was. She could picture Blake as a small bewildered boy, shattered by the grief of losing his mother, struggling to support his grieving father, only to lose his family home. No wonder he was so determined to get it back. He couldn't bring his mother back but this was one thing he could do. 'Did your father ever remarry or—?'

The rueful twist was back on his mouth. 'He hasn't even been on a date.'

The strength of Blake's father's love for his mother made what she'd felt for Simon look like a schoolgirl crush.

Maybe that was what it had been...

'He must have loved her so very much.'

Blake's eyes moved away from hers, a frown settling between his brows. 'I wouldn't have thought it was possible to love someone that much if I hadn't witnessed it first-hand. He literally couldn't function without her. He barely functions now, especially after his recent heart surgery. He wouldn't have needed it if he'd been taking better care of himself over the years. But I'm hoping getting this place back for him will be a step in the right direction.'

'You're doing it for *him*?' Tillie asked.

His gaze came back to hers, a cynical smile tilting the edges of his mouth. 'What? Did you think I wanted to set up a playboy mansion for myself?'

She bit her bottom lip. That was exactly what

she'd thought. 'It was an easy assumption to make, especially the way you went about it. Demanding I pretend to be your fiancée as if I would jump at the chance.'

He gave a soft grunt that might have been his version of an apology. 'I see you're still wearing my ring.'

'That's because the only way to get it off would be cut it or my finger off.'

There was another moment or two of silence.

Tillie started sweeping away invisible crumbs. 'I've been thinking about this arrangement we have between us…' she began.

Blake's gaze was steady and watchful. 'And?'

She licked the sudden dryness off her lips. 'Well, I might be mistaken about this but I got the feeling when you kissed me the other—'

'Don't do this—'

'Thing is… I haven't had a relationship… I mean a physical relationship…so—'

'No.' The word was flatly delivered, sounding like a punctuation mark driven in by the very determined nib of a pen.

Why did he keep saying no?

Tillie took a moment to pick up her splintered ego. 'Why is that? Because you don't fancy me or—?'

He rose from the chair with a jerky movement.

'I'm not going to sleep with you, Tillie. It wouldn't be…right.'

'Oh, so you've suddenly developed a conscience, have you?' Tillie said. 'Pity you didn't have one with you when you blackmailed me into being your fiancée.'

His jaw grew tense as if he was biting down on his molars. 'My *pretend* fiancée. I'm not intending it to become official. One month, that's all. One month.'

'Did I say I wanted you to make it official?'

His frown flickered as if not sure whether to deepen or relax. 'What exactly do you want?'

Did he have to make her spell it out? 'I just thought since we…erm…got on okay you might be able to help me with my…erm…little problem.'

His eyes were the darkest she had ever seen them, a smoky grey as deep and mysterious as the lake outside. 'What little problem?'

Tillie interlaced her hands in front of her body, reminding herself of when she was a tongue-tied schoolgirl standing in front of a stern headmaster over a uniform code violation. 'As you said the other day, it's unusual for a woman of my age to still be a virgin, so… I wondered…if you would consider helping me to not be a virgin any more.'

There was an echoing silence.

Blake's frown dug a deep trench between his

eyes. 'You're not serious…*are you*?' The incred-
ulous tone of his voice made it sound as if she
were asking him to make a human sacrifice of
her and then grind her blood and bones and feed
them to the jackdaws.

'Of course I'm serious,' Tillie said. 'I'm sick of
being a virgin. I only agreed to remain celibate
for Simon's sake and then he went off and had
sex with someone else behind my back. That's
what made me the angriest. Do you know how
that made me feel? Worthless, that's how. Hid-
eously undesirable and worthless.'

Blake drew in a breath and then released it in
a ragged stream. 'Look, here's the thing. I admit
I was thinking about sleeping with you, seriously
thinking about it, but when I found out you hadn't
been with a guy before it changed everything.
I'm not the white-picket-fence man you're after.
It would be wrong to sleep with you knowing I
couldn't offer you the whole package.'

'But I don't want the whole package,' Tillie
said. 'Been there, done that, got the wedding
dress and cake to prove it.'

His frown resembled isobar patterns on a map.
'What are you saying? You don't want to get married one day and have a family?'

Tillie wasn't so sure about the family part. She
hadn't quite ruled out a rosy-cheeked kid or two.

With IVF technology women didn't need a husband to become a mother. But marriage she had ruled out with a thick red pen. 'I'm open about having a child but not about having a husband. I can safely say no man will ever get me to put on a white dress and veil and turn up at church ever again.'

'People don't always get married in a church—'

'It's not the venue that's the problem,' Tillie said. 'It's the institution of marriage I'm shying away from. I want to have the life I missed out on while I was saving myself for Simon. I want to make up for all the opportunities I lost.'

Blake rubbed a hand down over his face until it distorted his features. 'This is crazy.'

Tillie wasn't sure what to make of his response. She'd thought—hoped—he'd jump at the chance to sleep with her. Now she wondered if it wasn't so much about her being a virgin but more about her being unattractive. All her self-doubt and insecurities came back like ants to a pile of spilled sugar. She wasn't model thin like the women he dated. She wasn't fashion conscious. She didn't wear enough make-up. She didn't show enough cleavage. The list went on and on.

'Fine,' she said. 'I get the message loud and clear. It was dumb of me to think someone like you might be remotely interested in someone like me.'

Blake came over to where she was standing and took her by the upper arms, his frowning gaze holding hers. 'You should think about this for a day or two before you rush into something you might regret.'

It was Tillie's turn to frown. 'Why would I regret doing what every other girl my age does without blinking an eye?'

His hands slipped away from her arms and he stepped back out of her personal space. 'I just think you need to put the brakes on, that's all.'

Tillie pressed her mouth flat, her arms folded in front of her. 'I'm starting to regret my invitation for you to come and stay here.'

'Is that why you issued it?' His tone had a sharp edge to it that scraped her already raw nerves. 'So I could help you with your "little problem", as you call it?'

'No. I do think you're right—people will wonder why if we're not under the same roof, especially since everyone knows you're not a saint. They expect us to be sleeping together. It wouldn't be normal for you not to.'

He pushed back his hair with a distracted hand. 'Just give it a day or two, okay? Think of it as a cooling-off period. The best business decisions are made that way.'

'Is that how you see this? As a business decision?'

A shutter came down at the back of his gaze like a vault being sealed off. 'My goal is and always has been to get this place back into my hands. You became a part of that plan when I struck that deal with you over the money you owed. But if you would prefer me to call our pretend engagement off then that's what I'll do. You won't owe me a penny. It's your choice.'

Was he testing her?

But even if he wasn't how could she walk away and see him lose the house he loved so much for a second time? He hadn't told her anything much about his mother, but the little he'd told her about his father made her realise how deeply he loved his dad and that he saw the return of the estate as essential to his well-being. She might have been able to walk away before, but not now. Not now she realised how important McClelland Park was to him and his hopes for his father's recovery.

'No. I want you to get your house back,' Tillie said. 'It's the right thing to do even if the way we're going about it is a little unconventional.'

If he gave a sigh of relief he hid it well for barely anything showed on his expression. 'Thank you.'

* * *

Blake brought his things in from the car while Tillie got working on dinner. A part of him insisted he repack the car and head out of that driveway before any more damage was done. But right then, her offer of a no-strings fling was far more tempting than the strength of his convictions. Would it be wrong to have a physical relationship with her?

He had never made love to a virgin before, but he knew enough about the female form to know the wrong handling or rushing her before she was ready could be not only painful but emotionally scarring as well. He hadn't thought he was one of those men who held female sexuality to different standards from men. He wasn't so draconian to think a woman was less of a person for having been sexually active. Sexual desire was a normal human process and why shouldn't women experience it in the same way men did without feeling guilty?

But the fact Tillie was a virgin did make him feel…special was not the right word. Privileged, honoured that she had decided to ask him to be her first partner. It wasn't because she held any true affection for him; he wouldn't agree to do it if she did. Feelings got in the way when it came to having casual sex. He was a master at blocking his. Now and again he would get the odd vague stirring over a particular partner, but he always moved on before it had time to take hold.

Tillie's attraction to him was purely physical—the best sort of attraction when it came to negotiating a no-strings fling. It wasn't as if his relationship with her was going to last longer than those he'd had with other women. A month was the longest he'd been involved with someone, although he had never cohabited with a partner before.

Would it be stepping over a boundary too far? Sharing a house this size shouldn't be an issue, but this wasn't just any house. This was a treasure trove of deeply emotional memories for him, a place where he had experienced love and happiness and a deep sense of belonging unlike anything in his life since.

Once Blake had put his things in the room Tillie had prepared, he walked a few metres further down the wide hall and opened the door of the bedroom he had occupied as a child. The bed, the furniture and curtains and paintwork were all different, leaving no trace of the boy who had spent the first ten years of his life there.

But when he walked over to the window and looked at the view, he was thrown back in time to that last day when he'd stood in this exact spot, his heart a bruising weight in his chest. From this window he could see the old elm tree with its limbs spread like the wings of a broody hen sheltering her chicks. He had carved his name where no one could see on that ancient elm tree that had watched over so many generations of McClellands.

His name written there was a secret promise to his ancestors that one day he would be back to claim the only true home he had ever known.

Tillie came up the stairs a while later to tell Blake dinner would be in ten minutes. She couldn't find him at first. He wasn't in the room she'd prepared for him, although his bags were. She walked further down the corridor and came to a smaller bedroom where she found him standing in front of the window with his hands in his trouser pockets, staring at the view of the lush green rolling fields and acres of woodland beyond.

He must have sensed her watching him for he turned and gave her a vague-looking smile as if he was lost in his thoughts. 'Sorry, did you say something?'

Tillie came further into the room, stopping when she got to just in front of him. It was hard to read his expression but she sensed he was struggling to keep his emotions locked away. 'Was this your bedroom when you were a boy?'

His eyes moved away from hers to gaze out of the window again. 'See that old elm tree in the distance?' He pointed to a gnarled tree Tillie had sat under many times playing with Truffles. She'd always thought it a magical sort of place, the kind of tree she had read about as a child in her favourite Enid Blyton books.

'Yes,' she said, acutely aware of the way his shirtsleeve brushed the bare skin of her arm as he pointed.

He dropped his hand, his gaze still on the elm. 'I broke my arm when I fell out of that tree when I was nine years old. I got the plaster taken off just before my tenth birthday.' He paused for a nanosecond. 'If only I had known that was the last birthday I would ever spend here with my mother.'

Tillie slipped her arm through his to offer what comfort she could. 'I'm sure your mother would be very proud of the man you've become, especially as you're doing all you can to help your dad.'

He made a sound that was somewhere between a sigh and a grunt. 'It would've broken her heart to know we had to leave this place.'

'It's an easy place to fall in love with.'

He turned and gave her one of his half-smiles. 'Where did you grow up?'

'Not in a place as nice as this,' Tillie said, slipping her arm out of his. 'We only ever lived in vicarages attached to parishes so I never knew any place as home in that sense. The longest we lived any place was right here in this village but that was only for four years before dad was transferred to another parish in Newcastle. That's why I stayed with Simon's parents because I didn't want to interrupt my final year of school. I secretly hoped my dad and stepmother would change their mind about going but they didn't seem too worried about leaving me behind. They aren't really interested in First World problems. They live by faith.'

His grey-blue eyes held hers. 'Did your father have to accept the transfer or could he have asked for an extension?'

Tillie had always struggled with her father's decision to move but, being an obedient daughter, had never said anything. It felt a little strange to be confessing what she felt about that time to someone as worldly as Blake. 'He would never have questioned the decision because he believed it was a calling. I had to accept it but I can't say it was easy.'

'Do you live by faith too?'

Tillie's look was sheepish. 'Please don't tell my father and stepmother but I'm not very good at it. I like to know there is plenty of money in the bank and that all the bills will be paid on time.'

'Seems fair enough to me.'

There was a little pause.

'What about you?' Tillie asked. 'Do you be-lieve in a higher power who is watching over you all the time?'

His eyes suddenly darkened and one of his hands went to her face and trailed a nerve-tingling pathway down the slope of her cheek. 'If there is, then what I'm about to do is going to send me straight to hell.'

Tillie disguised a gulping swallow. 'Wh-what are you going to do?'

'Guess,' he said and brought his mouth down to hers.

CHAPTER SIX

BLAKE'S LIPS WERE strong, determined—hard, almost. As if he resented the attraction he felt for her and was fighting it to the last. Tillie didn't want him to fight it, she wanted him to embrace it the way she was embracing the fiery attraction she felt for him. The heat in his mouth spread to hers like combustible fuel, sending tingling sparks of feeling from the nerves of her lips that travelled through her body like flicking, licking flames. His tongue found hers in a single thrust, curling, duelling, teasing it into intimate play.

She pressed her body into his tall, hard frame, opening her mouth to his exploration, her tongue becoming bolder with every heart-stopping second. He tasted of mint and coffee and desperation, his lips moving on hers with exquisite expertise until her senses were singing like a symphony choir. How could a kiss stir her into such raptures of feeling? The sensations travelled in a hot rush from her mouth to her core as if his kiss had programmed a secret pathway through her body.

His hands went to her hips, holding her against the surge of his male flesh, leaving her in no doubt the desire she was experiencing was in no way one-sided. His body was as turned on as hers.

He lifted his mouth off hers to blaze a trail of kisses down the side of her neck. 'You have to tell me to stop.' There was almost a pleading note to his tone but there was no way she was going to do any such thing.

Tillie traced the dip in his chin below his mouth where his stubble was rich and dense and arrantly male. 'What if I don't want you to stop?'

His hands tightened on her hips, his eyes pools of smouldering smoky grey. 'You're not making this easy for me.'

She lifted up on tiptoe to press her mouth to his in a series of feather-light touchdowns. 'I want you to make love to me.'

His mouth responded by kissing her with the same hot pressure, making every nerve in her lips tingle. 'I've wanted you since the first day you served me in the shop.'

Tillie pressed another kiss to his mouth. 'Why? Because of my chocolate éclairs?'

He smiled against her mouth. 'That and other things.'

She eased back to look up at him. 'What other things?'

He sent a lazy fingertip over the shape of her eyebrows. 'When you handed me my change, I knew we would be dynamite together.'

So he'd felt that zapping tingle, too? Tillie had tried not to touch him all the times she'd served him since but he always made sure their hands came into contact. Was that why he always insisted on being served by her and not Joanne? 'Did you eat all those éclairs or were they just a ruse to get my attention?'

He gave her a crooked smile. 'Of course I ate them. There's only so much temptation a man can stand.' He brushed a strand of hair off her face. 'Are you sure about this? Really sure?'

Tillie slid her hands up his chest to link her arms around his neck. 'Absolutely.' She leaned closer, pressing her breasts into the wall of his chest, her mouth connecting with his in an explosive kiss as if the final bolt on his restraint had popped.

His hands cupped her bottom to hold her to his hard heat, his tongue tangling with hers in a sexy dance that made her insides shudder in delight.

This was how a kiss was meant to be: passionate, unstoppable. Irresistible.

Tillie sucked in a breath when one of his hands moved from her bottom to slide up to just below her breast. It was as thrilling as if he had cupped it naked in his hand. But he seemed to be taking care not to rush her and instead kept kissing her slowly in a way that made her senses swoon as if she'd been given a powerful drug. She made little noises under the sensual play of his mouth, greedy, needy noises that signalled her desire for him as blatantly as the surge of his body against hers. Never had she felt anything like this tumultuous fever in her flesh. Every nerve of her body was activated, on high alert, anticipating the next brush of his mouth, the next glide of his hand, the ultimate possession of his body moving with heat and urgency within hers.

Blake walked her backwards to the bed, his mouth still locked on hers in a blistering kiss that made the base of her belly quiver like an unset jelly. His tongue was moving in and out of her mouth in an erotic mimic of his carnal intent.

Tillie began to work on his clothes, keen to get her hands on his naked flesh. She undid a couple of buttons on his shirt but her fingers were all but useless. He undid the rest and hauled it over his head and tossed it to the floor beside the bed. She planted her hands on his chest, running her palms over his toned muscles, wondering again where he'd stored all those calories she'd sold him.

Sudden shyness gripped her.

Would the little bulge of her tummy that no amount of sit-ups had ever been able to shift put him off? Her dimpled thighs? What if he was completely turned off by her body? She wasn't anything like the svelte model types he dated.

He must have sensed her change of mood for he stilled his movements and searched her gaze. 'It's not too late to change your mind.'

Tillie lowered her eyes and snagged her lower lip with her teeth. 'It's not that…'

He cupped her cheek in one warm dry hand, holding her gaze steady. 'Are you nervous?'

'A little…'

His thumb began a slow stroking motion across her cheek. 'You're a beautiful, sexy woman, Tillie. You have no need to doubt yourself.'

Was he a mind-reader or what?

'I've always been a bit self-conscious about my body,' Tillie said. 'Simon made it worse by insisting I cover it up all the time. I started to see it as problematic, something to be ashamed of, to hide away instead of being proud of my curves.'

Blake's hand gently cupped her breast through

her clothes. 'I've been having fantasies about your curves since the first day I met you.'

'You have?'

His eyes gave a sexy twinkle and he started to undo the buttons on her top. Her skin tingled when his fingers brushed against her and her inner core clenched with a spasm of desire so strong it threatened to take her legs out from under her. He peeled away her dress and let it fall to the floor next to his shirt. His fingertip skated over the twin upper curves of her breasts still encased in her bra. The sensation of his finger grazing her was electrifying, making her nipples stand up and cry, *Touch me!*

'So beautiful.' His voice was a low deep murmur that made her skin break out in goose bumps. Then he bent his head and sent his tongue over each of her breasts in a slow lick that made her spine feel as if someone had undone each and every one of her vertebrae. Who knew there were so many nerves in her breasts? That the lazy stroke of his tongue would make her tingle from the top of her head to the balls of her feet?

Tillie heard a pleading sound and then realised it had come from her. His teeth grazed her nipple in a gentle bite that made her hair lift away from her scalp. His tongue circled, tracing the darker skin of her areole and then moving to the sensitive underside of her breast. He did the same to her other breast, pushing it up to meet his mouth with one of his hands, the sensations so powerful, so entrancing her whole body quivered. Need clawed at her insides, clenching, aching need that was being fuelled by every touch and press of his mouth and hands.

He moved down her body, kissing her sternum, her belly button, gently peeling away her knickers so he could access her most intimate flesh. She automatically tensed, but he calmed her by placing his hand on her stomach just above her mound, soothing her as a trainer did a flighty horse. 'Relax, sweetheart. I won't hurt you.'

Tillie slowly let out the breath she was holding, forcing her spine to ease back against the mattress. He began to stroke her with his fingertips, gauging her response, encouraging her to tell him what worked and what didn't. And she would have told him if she'd been capable of speech. All she could manage was a breathless gasp as her sensitive nerves flickered like a struck match. He brought his mouth to her and began a slow exploration of her, soft little licks and nudges opening her like a flower, allowing her time to get used to his touch, to the feel of his breath moving over her.

The sensations were building in a powerful

wave, pulling all her flesh to one single delicious point at the swollen heart of her body. She could even feel the tension in the arches of her feet. It was like a terrifyingly savage storm approaching. She felt it coming but pulled back from it, afraid of its impact on her, of what it would do and how, or even whether, she could control it.

'Go with it, Tillie,' Blake said. 'Don't be frightened of it.'

'I—I can't.' She put a hand up to cover her face, suddenly embarrassed at how gauche she must seem to him.

He gently brought her hand away and gave it a soft squeeze. 'You're doing fine. It's hard to orgasm with a partner for the first time. But I've got you. I won't let anything bad happen to you. Roll with it. Let it take you.'

Tillie lay back and closed her eyes, letting him caress her with his lips and tongue. It was as if he was reading her body, letting it tell him what it needed. The pressure built again and this time there was no escaping the waves of pleasure, they seemed to crash into her and over her, spinning her into a vortex where she was beyond thought, her body so intensely captivated by feelings she had never experienced with such spectacular force before. Cascading, undulating waves moved through her body, leaving her limbless, boneless in the golden aftermath.

Blake stroked the flank of her thigh. 'See? I knew you could do it.'

Tillie reached for him, drawing him closer so she could touch him. 'That was…amazing. But you have too many clothes on.'

'I got a little distracted there for a moment.' He stood from the bed and slipped out of his trousers and undershorts, before reaching for a condom from his wallet.

He came back to her on the bed, lying beside her so as not to overwhelm her. 'We don't have to do this if you don't feel ready.'

Tillie stroked his length. 'I'm ready. More than ready.'

I've been ready since the day I met you.

His features flickered with pleasure as her hand began moving up and down his shaft. The erotic power of him thrilled her, making her inner core tighten in anticipation. 'Am I doing it right?' she asked.

'You can do it harder. You won't hurt me.'

She squeezed her fingers around him and moved faster, delighting in the way his breathing changed. He brought his mouth down to hers, kissing her long and deep, his tongue mating with hers in a sexy mimic of what was to come.

Tillie moved her pelvis against him, letting her body communicate its need. He positioned himself over her, taking his weight on his arms so as not to crush her, his legs angled around hers.

He brushed her hair back from her face, his eyes dark with desire. 'Still okay with this? It's not too late to say no.'

Tillie touched his face, the rasp of his stubble against her fingertips reminding her of how different his body was from hers. 'I want you.'

He dropped a soft kiss to her lips. 'I want you, too.' Then he slowly moved against her entrance, allowing her the feel of him without going any further. 'Tell me if I'm hurting you.'

Tillie brought her hand to him to guide him, not that he needed any directing. He was being so considerate but her body didn't want his consideration. It wanted him. Now.

He glided in a short distance, giving her time to get used to him. Then he moved deeper within her, a little bit at a time until she was comfortable with his presence. 'Still okay?' he asked.

'More than okay,' Tillie said, stroking her hands over his back and shoulders. 'You feel amazing.'

'You feel pretty damn amazing yourself.' He brushed her lips with his, softly and then with firmer pressure as if the need pounding in him was urging him on.

It was urging her, too. The primal power of it was surging through her body, making her gasp and groan and whimper as he began a slow rhythm of thrusting and retreating and then thrusting again.

There was none of the awkwardness she'd been expecting. None of the shame about her not so perfect body. She was swept up in the magical momentum of discovering the pleasure spots and erogenous zones of her body and feeling proud of how it responded to him. Like how her breasts became super-sensitive when he swirled his tongue around and over her nipples. Like how her neck and underneath her earlobes had thousands of nerves that danced and leapt under the glide and stroke of his mouth and tongue.

Tillie could feel her body swelling with need, a deep ache throbbing in her flesh, but she was unable to get to the final moment of lift off. She moved beneath him, searching for that little bit extra friction, finding it and then losing it just when she needed it most. 'I can't… I can't…'

'Yes, you can,' he said and brought one of his hands down between their bodies and stroked her intimately. It was all she needed to fly. The shimmering, shuddering sensations ricocheting through her from head to toe, leaving no part of her unaffected. She clung to him while the tumult thrashed her about, digging her fingers into his buttocks, feeling a little shocked by the way her body was so out of her control. Making love with someone was so different from self-pleasure. The skin-on-skin contact, the scent of arousal, the giving and receiving of pleasure made the experience so much more satisfying.

Blake waited until she was coming out of her orgasm before he took his own pleasure. She felt each of his shudders, heard his guttural groan that seemed to come from a deep dark cavern inside him. The power of it moving through him amazed her. Had he experienced the same earth-shattering sensations? Had she really done that to him?

He lifted his head and met her gaze. 'It will get better the more we do it.'

Tillie traced the line of his lower lip. 'I can't imagine how it could get better for me. I didn't know my body was capable of that.'

'You have a beautiful body that is capable of dismantling every bit of self-control I muster.'

She searched his face for a beat or two. 'Was it good for you?'

He pressed a kiss to her mouth. 'Better than good. Amazing. I've never slept with anyone like you before.'

'You mean a virgin?'

He played with a stray strand of her hair, winding it around his finger and letting it go, only to wind it back up again. 'Not just that.'

'Because I'm fat?'

A frown formed between his eyes. 'You aren't fat. You've got a gorgeous figure.'

'Have all your other lovers been slim?'

He did a slow blink and let out a long breath as if summoning his patience. Then he rolled away and dealt with the condom before he sat on the edge of the bed, one of his hands coming to rest on the side of her thigh. 'Listen to me, Tillie.' His voice had that stern schoolmaster tone going on. 'I understand that years of being engaged to a guy who never even tried to consummate the relationship would do a fair bit of damage to a girl's self-esteem. But I hate hearing you being so negative about your body. You have nothing to be ashamed of.'

Tillie let out a sigh. 'I'm sorry for spoiling the moment.'

He gave her a half-smile and leaned down to press another kiss to her mouth. 'Repeat after me. I am beautiful just the way I am.'

She turned her head away. 'No! That sounds so ridiculously vain.'

Blake turned her face back so she had to meet his gaze. 'Say it.'

Tillie looked into his eyes and for the first time in her life felt beautiful. Beautiful and desirable. 'I am beautiful just the way I am. There, I said it. Now will you let me go?'

He trailed a lazy fingertip down between her breasts. 'Is that what you want me to do? Let you go or play with you some more?'

A shiver raced over Tillie's flesh at the sexy glint in his eyes. 'You want me again?'

He took one of her hands and brought it to the swell of his erection. 'You turn me on, Tillie Toppington. Big time.'

She stroked the proud heft of him, delighting in the way his expression contorted with each movement of her hand. 'Will you promise to stop treating me like I'm made of glass?'

'Are you sore?'

Tillie squeezed her legs together but while there was a slight twinge it was more pleasure than pain. 'Not a bit.'

He came back down beside her, lying on his side with one elbow propping him up. His other hand slowly caressed her thigh, a small frown interrupting his features. 'I was so determined I wasn't going to do this. I don't want you to get the wrong idea about us going forward—'

Tillie pressed a fingertip to his lips to silence him. 'Will you repeat after me? I am having a no-strings fling with you and I am completely okay about it.'

His expression flickered as if he was struggling with his conscience. 'I'm having a no-strings fling with you and I am completely okay about it.'

'You don't sound very convincing,' Tillie said, stroking the crease of his frown away without much success. 'Your eyes were saying, *what the hell have I done?*'

His mouth tilted in a rueful manner but his eyes still contained smoky grey shadows. 'As long as we're both clear on the boundaries.'

'I'm perfectly clear on the boundaries,' Tillie said, holding her fingers up as if to check off a list. 'We are going to have heaps of hot sex. We are not going to fall in love. And as soon as you get McClelland Park back we will end our fling.'

He tapped her on the end of her nose. '*You* will end it.'

'Oh, yes. I get to do the honours this time,' Tillie said. 'Will I do it in person or would you prefer a text?'

His frown came back. 'If ever I run into your ex I'm going to tell him what a pathetic yellow-bellied coward he is.'

Tillie couldn't help feeling a thrill at his comment. While everyone in the village had supported her in her disappointment when Simon jilted her, her father and stepmother had taken the 'forgive and forget' approach. Their lack of anger at Simon had made her feel as if they weren't listening to her, as if they were completely unaware of how deeply hurt she felt about being left in the lurch like that.

'You know something?' she said, toying with a whorl of Blake's chest hair as if it was the most fascinating thing she had ever seen, which, quite frankly, it was. Simon hadn't had a single hair on his chest and not from waxing them off, either. 'I was really disappointed when my father and stepmother refused to be angry with Simon. They kept carrying on about how I should forgive and forget as if he'd simply cancelled a date. I found it upsetting they thought it was far more important to forgive him than to let me express how hurt I was. I stopped talking to them about it because I know it disappointed them to see me so bitter and angry.'

Why are you telling him all your stuff?

Tillie knew exactly why. Because he listened with a concerned look on his face as if he were putting himself in her shoes and feeling hurt and betrayed on her behalf.

'Are you close to them?'

Tillie had always thought she was up until Simon had jilted her. 'I was hurt by the way they hadn't seemed to fully understand how devastated I was the day of the wedding. I expected them to be furious on my behalf. They had flown thousands of miles to be there, and at great cost, and yet when it was called off they simply shrugged as if a tea party had been cancelled.'

His expression was not only concerned but she was almost certain she could see a flicker of anger lurking in the back of his gaze. Anger on her behalf. 'That's terrible. They should've supported you better than that. Don't they know you at all?'

What was he saying? That *he* knew her better than her own family? Weird. Nice weird. 'I guess if I was truly close to them I would have told them the truth about you and me. But I didn't. I didn't feel comfortable lying to them but it was easier than admitting I was pretending to be engaged. They hold marriage as sacred so it would appal them that I was acting the part of your fiancée with no intention of it ever being real.'

Blake's frown dug a little deeper on his brow. 'What will they think of us living together?'

'I'm not sure they'll find out unless someone else in the village mentions it if they were to write or email them. I only told them we were engaged. They're on a remote mission posting in Uganda. The Internet and phone coverage is patchy and unreliable so I haven't heard back yet. Sometimes it can take days or even weeks to hear back from them.'

He threaded his fingers through hers, bringing up her hand to his mouth, holding her gaze with his thoughtful and serious one. 'It's never been my intention to come between you and your family.'

'You're doing no such thing,' Tillie said. 'I'm not a child. I'm twenty-four years old and if I want to live with a man for a few weeks then that's my business.'

'You're not worried they might be disappointed you didn't—?'

'What? Wait for another Simon to come along and keep me in an ivory tower for years and years only to run off with someone else?' she said. 'No, thanks. I'm done with weddings.'

'So what's with the wedding cake in your back room at the shop?'

'I'm using it as therapy. I figure it's cheaper than seeing a therapist. Every day I stick a dressmaking pin into Simon's marzipan figure.'

'Is it helping?'

Tillie thought about it for a moment. Funny,

but she hadn't stuck a pin in Simon since Blake had 'proposed' to her. 'Yes and no. I still have to do something about the wedding dress. It's taking up too much room in the wardrobe. It's like a cumulonimbus cloud crammed in there. I've thought of selling it, but I think it would be much more satisfying to cut it into ribbons.'

A flicker of amusement flirted with his mouth, but then his expression became serious again. 'Jim Pendleton told me you didn't get much say in choosing it.'

'No…but that was my fault for not standing up to Simon's mother,' Tillie said. 'That's the problem with wanting to belong to someone. You don't just belong to them but to their family, too. But I can see now Marilyn never accepted me as a future daughter-in-law. Nor did Simon's father. They tolerated me. I can't help wondering how they're getting on with his new partner.'

'Would you ever go back to him if he—?'

'No. Absolutely not.'

Blake's frown hadn't quite left his forehead. He traced a pathway around her mouth with one of his fingertips. 'You were too good for him. Way too good.'

Tillie screwed up her face and then tiptoed her fingers down his sternum. 'I wish you'd stop calling me good. I want to be bad.'

His smile ignited a spark in his eyes and he brought his mouth down to hers. 'That's what I'm here for, sweetheart.'

CHAPTER SEVEN

BLAKE KISSED HIS way down her body, his hormones going nuts over the swell and shape of her curves. Why had he always dated stick insects when he could have had this? Her body was his every secret fantasy. The way she responded to him, the way she moved against him, the way she held him as if she never wanted to let him go. He couldn't remember a time when sex had been more satisfying.

Or more terrifying.

He had been so determined to keep control all the way through but in the end he'd blown like a bomb. That she could do that to him was a little unnerving. He was supposed to be the one at the control panels but every time his mouth met hers, he felt that control slip further out of his reach.

He came down to her breasts and swirled his tongue over her right nipple, taking the tight bud gently between his teeth, his blood pounding in his groin when she gave a breathless little gasp and clutched at his shoulders as if torn between wanting more and pushing him away.

He knew the feeling. The tug of war between common sense and a desire so raw and primal it took control of his flesh, made him a pawn to its needs—needs that he normally had firm discipline over, but not now. Not with her.

This was different.

Tillie was different.

She awakened something in him that up until now had been lying dormant.

He liked the closeness of making love to her. Coaching her into the magic of physical pleasure had intensified his own. He felt sensations he had never felt before. He had let go in a way he never had before. He hadn't had any choice. It was as if her body had triggered something in his—something dark and unknowable, a force he had fooled himself he didn't possess.

But it was there.

Lurking deep and secretively inside him.

The need to be close to someone, not just physically but enough to tell them about the things that weighed him down or buoyed him up.

When Tillie had told him how disappointed she'd been when her father and stepmother hadn't seemed to understand her devastation at being jilted, he'd felt a striking sense of commonality. A bond he hadn't felt with anyone else. The sense that someone else understood isolation and loneliness. Understood the hurt that couldn't be erased with a few casually flung platitudes.

Tillie was nursing her own hurt, but was a fling with him the way to go about eradicating it? She said she no longer wanted the fairy tale. Could he believe she had changed so much in a matter of months? She still had her wedding cake and dress, for God's sake. She might say she was keeping them as part of her getting-over-her-ex therapy, but how sure could he be she was telling the truth? Even to herself?

He knew all about the lies people told themselves when they didn't want to face stuff. Hadn't he been lying to himself all these years about his father? Thinking, hoping that *this* year things would be different. Better. That his dad would finally emerge out of the well of grief he'd been drowning in for the last twenty-four years.

But had it happened?

Not yet, but Blake was determined he would make it happen.

Tillie's hand glided over his chest, her mouth fused to his in a passionate kiss that made the base of his spine tingle. She made soft little whimpering noises and opened her mouth for the entry of his tongue. Her tongue played with his in a dart and retreat dance that made the blood in his veins pound. What was it about her mouth that made kissing so damn exciting? Every nerve in his lips was on high alert, the shape and mould of her mouth against his delighting him as if this was his first ever kiss. He could feel every movement of it as if it had been magnified through his senses. The way she licked his lower lip and then took it between her teeth in a kittenish bite, before releasing it to sweep her tongue back over it, made every other kiss he'd experienced feel like a platonic peck in comparison.

Her touch was soft and yet electric, her hands moving over his body in an almost worshipful manner. His skin lifted in goose bumps when she sent her hand down in search of his erection. Her shyness was as endearing as it was exciting. But there was nothing lacking in her caressing of him. She responded to his sounds of pleasure as if they had their own secret language that no one else knew. Reading his body, stroking it with increasing confidence and boldness, making his senses go haywire.

Blake pulled away so he could concentrate on giving her pleasure. He moved down her body, kissing her stomach and then lower to her feminine mound. She was so responsive to him, so relaxed now under his touch it made him feel a level of trust had developed between them unlike anything he had experienced in his other relationships.

With Tillie, sex wasn't just sex. It was a discovery of the senses, a sensual journey with unexpected and thrilling results.

She came under the ministrations of his tongue, her hands gripping his head to anchor herself until the storm abated. 'Wow…just wow…' she said, her cheeks and décolletage still flushed with pleasure.

Blake smiled and moved up her body, turning her so she was straddling him. He reached for a condom but before he could put it on, she took it from him.

'Let me,' she said.

He glided his hands up and down her arms while she put the condom on him with smooth strokes down his shaft that nearly took the top of his head off. She wriggled her body, taking him deep inside with a part-groan, part-gasp that thrilled him as much as the feel of her body gripping him so tightly. 'This way you can set the pace,' he said. 'Slow or fast, whatever you need.'

'I need you.' She lowered her face to his to kiss him.

Blake feasted on her mouth, tangling his tongue with hers, his lower body in raptures over what was going on down there. Tillie was riding him slowly, moving her body up and down and round and round until he was fighting to stay in control. Being able to see her joined to him so intimately ramped up his excitement. The pleasure rippling through him was played out on her features as if their bodies were tuned to report what each was feeling.

'You can do it,' he said when he could see she was close to orgasm. 'Don't hold back.'

She gave a sharp cry and then shuddered and shook over him, triggering his own release until his groans joined hers. Finally, she slumped over his still-tingling body, her hair tickling his face and neck, her chest rising and falling against his.

He stroked the silky-smooth skin of her back, enjoying the feel of her curves pressing into the harder planes of his body. 'You're not going to go all shy on me now, are you?' he said.

Tillie turned her head so she could access his neck, sending her tongue out to lick just below his ear. 'I did feel a little bit…exposed doing it like that.'

Blake turned his head to look at her. 'You look beautiful when you come.'

Her cheeks went a faint shade of pink and her

fingertip came up and passed over his stubbled jaw all the way to his mouth, her gaze lowered to follow its pathway. 'I knew sex would be good, but I didn't realise it would be this good.'

He lifted his hand to sweep her disordered hair back off her face. 'It's not always this good.'

Her eyes flickered with surprise. 'Even for you, you mean?'

'Yeah,' he said, realising with a strange little jolt it was true. 'Even for me.'

She propped herself up on her elbows, her eyes meeting his and her naked breasts with their tightly budded nipples tantalising him all over again. 'I have nothing to compare it with other than…you know…' Her cheeks fired up again and her gaze slipped out of reach of his.

Blake brought her chin up with the end of his finger. 'There's nothing to be ashamed about. Self-pleasure is the key to finding out what works for you and what doesn't and it's particularly important for women.'

She pressed her lips together for a moment. 'I know…but it's hard to shake off the repressed attitudes you've grown up with. I often wondered if it was somehow breaking the abstinence rule.'

'Is that what your ex thought?'

'Simon hardly ever talked about things like that,' she said with a little laugh. 'I asked him once if he ever relieved himself but he got all touchy about it, saying it was wrong of me to talk about sex when he was trying not to think about it.'

Blake frowned. 'And you were seriously going to marry this guy?'

Tillie's mouth flattened and two little circles of pink formed on her cheeks. She moved away from him and went in search of her clothes. 'I know it's probably hard for someone like you to understand my reasons for wanting to be with Simon, but—'

'Why someone like me?' Blake asked, swinging his legs over the side of the bed.

She snatched up her clothes and held them against the front of her body. 'You're good-looking and successful and can have anyone you want. It's different for people like me.'

'I'm not following you,' Blake said. 'You have just as much right to a good relationship as anyone else. Why would you settle for anything less?'

She sent him a pointed glance. 'Why do you settle for casual relationships and not something a little more lasting?'

He kept his expression blank. 'We're not talking about me. We're talking about you.'

She slipped her dress over her head without putting on her bra, smoothing the fabric over her hips that minutes ago had been pressed against his. Her features relaxed on a confessional sigh. 'I was never the popular girl at school. I made friends easily enough, but because we moved every few years I had to leave them and start all over again. I taught myself to fit in where I could.'

'That would've been tough on a shy girl.'

Tillie gave a little you-can-say-that-again eye-roll. 'It was. But when I met Simon when I was sixteen…well, I gravitated towards him because he seemed sensible compared to the other boys at school. He wasn't into drugs or partying and he had strong values. He was conservative, yes, but I liked that about him. It was what I grew up with so it was familiar. We started hanging out together and then we became a couple and were together until the day of the wedding.'

'When did he propose to you?'

She bit down on her lower lip and averted her gaze to scoop up her knickers off the floor. She bundled them into a ball and held them in one hand. 'When I was twenty-one, but it wasn't a proposal as such…more like a discussion.'

'You never had doubts he wasn't the right one for you? Especially given his parents were mostly negative about you?'

A shadow of something that looked like regret passed over her face. 'Looking back, I think I ignored all the things that weren't working between us and focussed on what was working. I wanted him to be my soul mate so I only looked for things to confirm that and disregarded anything that didn't.' She did a cute little self-deprecating lip twist and asked, 'I guess you don't believe in everyone having a soul mate?'

Blake thought of his father and mother. They had been a solid unit, a perfectly balanced couple who had always brought out the best in each other. He often wondered if things had happened the other way around—his father dying instead of his mother—would his mother have struggled as much as his father? He got off the bed and stepped back into his trousers. 'If there is such a thing, I'm not sure I'd want one for myself.'

'Why not?'

Blake shrugged, wishing he'd kept his mouth shut. 'I just don't, that's all.'

Her smooth brow furrowed into fine lines. 'Because of what happened to your father when your mother died?'

Bang on the money, sweetheart.

He kept his expression masked but he could feel Tillie's brown gaze bearing down on his resolve to keep that part of his life closed off like a persistent file picking at a lock. 'Hey, I thought you were going to cook me dinner?' He kept his tone light, even managed to crank out a smile.

She continued to hold his gaze. 'You don't like talking about her, do you?'

Damn right I don't.

What good did talking do? It hadn't changed a thing in twenty-four years. As far as he was concerned, two people had been put in that coffin that day and he had been left to carry on alone. His dad had all but died with his mother and Blake had had to grow up overnight. He had borne way too much responsibility for a child of that age.

And that responsibility had continued well on into adulthood.

He didn't tie himself down to any one place or any one person because of it. For he knew, at a moment's notice, his dad might need him.

He never wanted to need someone like that.

As his dad had needed his mum. Having a soul mate might sound great in theory, but in practice it sucked if and when that person left you or died.

Blake was the one who left his relationships. He started them. He ended them. He moved on from them without regret.

But something about Tillie's gaze got to him. The way it was both soft and direct, as if she knew how painful his past was and yet was determined to get him to air it like a musty sweater that had been shoved at the back of the wardrobe.

He let out a long sigh that made something tightly knotted in his chest loosen just a fraction. 'No. I don't.'

Tillie came over to sit on the bed right in front of where he was standing, looking up at him with those doe eyes. In spite of the sombre nature of their conversation, he couldn't stop thinking about the fact she wasn't wearing underwear under her dress.

'I've often wondered if it's harder to lose a mother you've never known or one you knew and loved,' she said.

Blake blinked away the memory of his mother's death. How he had stood outside ICU the day her life support machine was turned off—because everyone had thought he was too young to be in there with her in her final moments—and prayed for and willed her to keep going even though the doctors said it was hopeless. But when his father had come out, Blake had known prayers rarely, if ever, got answered.

But then he thought of what Tillie said, and realised she must have lost her mother even earlier.

'It's hard on both counts,' he said. 'At least I have some memories. Do you have any of your mother?'

Her mouth rearranged itself into a wistful, almost-smile and her fingers absently plucked at the bedcover. 'She died within hours of my birth. I know it sounds a bit weird since I don't remember her at all, but I miss her. I miss the concept of her. My stepmother is lovely and all that but she can't tell me what it was like to carry me for nine months. What it was like to find out she was pregnant and all the hopes and dreams she had for me while she carried me in her womb. No one can do that but my actual mum. Every time Mother's Day comes around I feel like something—someone— is missing. It used to be awful at school when we made gifts for Mother's Day. I was always the only one without a mum. I would always make something I could leave on her grave, flowers and card or, once, a little pottery vase. Not that we visited her grave much. I think my dad found it difficult. Understandable, I guess. It wouldn't have been easy to lose his young wife that way.'

'Do you have any half-siblings from your father's marriage to your stepmother?'

'No. My stepmother couldn't have children,' Tillie said. 'She was so grateful for the chance to be a mum to a small child. I'm sure she was more in love with me than my dad at first.'

'Are they still happy?'

'Very,' she said. 'They have a lot in common.

They both have strong faith and love working abroad on the mission field. They both felt called to do it since childhood.'

There was a small silence.

'I couldn't drag my father away from my mother's grave the first time we visited after the funeral,' Blake said. 'I didn't come with him much after that. I couldn't bear seeing him in so much distress. Once I was old enough to drive I came alone. I felt guilty about it. I still feel guilty about it, but I just couldn't hack it. Every birthday, every Christmas, every anniversary, every excuse he could think of, he'd want me to come down with him. I would've gone if I'd thought it was helping him. But I had my doubts.'

Tillie stood from the bed and slipped one of her hands into one of his. 'You shouldn't feel guilty. You did all you could to support him. Anyway, you were just a child. And having to be strong all the time wouldn't have helped your own grieving process.'

'No,' Blake said, vaguely registering how good…how *freeing* it felt to talk so openly about something he had locked away for so long. 'It didn't. I couldn't mention my mother without it causing my dad to fall into a deep depression that would last for days, if not weeks. I more or less taught myself not to think about her. It was as if she had never existed.'

Tillie moved closer so that the front of her body brushed against his, her arms going around his waist. 'Thanks for telling me about her.'

Blake wrapped his arms around her to draw her closer, resting his chin on the top of her head. 'It felt good. I haven't spoken to anyone about her, including my father, for a long time.'

She tilted her head back to look at him. 'Does he know you're trying to buy back McClelland Park for him?'

'No, I'm keeping that as a surprise,' Blake said. 'I didn't want to get his hopes up if it falls through. But I think it will be the key to his full recovery. He never forgave himself for losing this place. If he gets it back, I'm hoping he'll get his mojo back as well and finally move on with his life.'

She stroked a hand from the hinge of his jaw to his chin. 'I hope Mr Pendleton sells it to you. He doesn't have a direct heir because his only daughter died when she was sixteen in a car accident with her boyfriend. He has a couple of nephews but they never visit him. I'm going to try and convince him you're the only one who should own McClelland Park.'

'Let's hope he agrees, otherwise all this will have been for nothing,' Blake said.

Something flickered across her features and her arms around his waist loosened slightly as if she was withdrawing from him. 'All this? You mean…us?'

Maybe his choice of words could have been a little better, but there was a part of him that felt worried he had stepped over a boundary too far. He gave her waist a quick squeeze before he released her from his hold, stepping back to allow her some space…or maybe it was him that needed space.

'I can't help feeling you're the one who's going to lose in the end,' he said.

'Why would you think that?' she said. 'We agreed on the terms. You paid off my debts so I would pretend to be your fiancée for a month and a month only. The only thing I've lost is my virginity, which is exactly what I wanted to lose.'

Blake searched her features for a long moment. Her eyes were clear and honest, her expression open and unguarded. Was he worrying about nothing? Why then this little niggling sense of unease? 'What if you fall in love with—?'

'Will you listen to yourself?' she said with a half-laugh. 'Does every woman you have a fling with fall in love with you?'

'No, but—'

'Then you don't have to worry about me.' She gave him a pert little glance. 'Or maybe it's not me you're worried about. Maybe it's you.'

Blake gave his own version of a that-will-never-happen-to-me laugh but somehow it didn't sound half as convincing as hers.

CHAPTER EIGHT

TILLIE AND BLAKE enjoyed dinner together in the dining room with Truffles sitting at Blake's elbow waiting politely for titbits. They hadn't returned to the subject of Blake's concern over her falling in love with him during the course of their short fling. She was quite proud of the way she'd handled his concern with a quip that flipped his question back at him.

She liked him.

She liked him a lot.

He was the dream fling partner: kind, funny, generous, sexy and intelligent. But falling in love was something she was guarding against. Blake wasn't interested in commitment and nor was she. She had spent too many years of her life in a relationship she believed was the real thing only for it to fall over when she least expected it.

Or had she expected it?

It was an unsettling thought, but a part of Tillie—a secret part—hadn't been one bit surprised when she'd received Simon's text just as she'd arrived at the church. Hadn't she felt for weeks, if not months, he was moving away from her? But she had doggedly continued with the wedding arrangements, ignoring the fact Simon wasn't as involved in the plans as he had been. That he spent more time at his parents' house than he did at the cottage with her. That he always had something pressing he had to see to on their date nights. All the clues were there but she had refused to see them. For the last three months she had been angry with him for leaving her, but now she was angry with herself for allowing things to go on so long without speaking up.

But not this time.

This time Tillie and Blake were in mutual agreement on the course of their fling. One month. No one was going to get hurt. No one was going to shift the goalposts. They were both gaining from the arrangement, and contrary to Blake's concerns, there wouldn't be a winner or a loser when it came time to end it.

But when Blake reached across to refill Tillie's wineglass, something about the way his grey-blue eyes caught hers made her heart trip like a foot missing a step. She glanced at his hands—those clever, capable hands that had explored every inch of her body—and her belly fluttered like a breeze moving over the pages of an open book. She pressed her knees together under the table, the tiny twinge of discomfort an erotic reminder of the workout her inner muscles had been given.

He must have read something on her expression for he put the wine bottle down and frowned. 'What's wrong, sweetheart?'

'Nothing.'

His frown stayed put and he narrowed his gaze and reached for her hand, stroking it so gently it was as if he were petting a tiny, much-adored kitten. 'Sure?'

Nerves Tillie hadn't even known she possessed danced under his touch. 'Do you know something funny? Simon always called me "dear". Like we were an old married couple in our eighties or something. It used to really annoy me, but for some reason I never said anything. Kind of pathetic, really.'

Blake's thumb stroked each tendon on her hand in turn. 'Why did you feel you couldn't express yourself with him?'

Tillie gave a one-shoulder shrug. 'I guess because deep down I was worried about him leaving me so I put up and shut up. I'm not going to make that mistake in future relationships. I'm going to speak up if something's worrying me.'

'Does it bother you when I call you sweetheart or babe?'

'No,' Tillie said. 'I like it. And anyway, you have to sound convincing if others are around so it's probably a good idea to keep doing it.'

'My dad called my mother darling,' he said after a long moment. 'I don't think I ever heard him call her Gwen—not until after she died.'

'What did she call him?'

A smile flickered across his mouth. 'She called him darling, too. But occasionally she called him Andrew if she was annoyed with him. Not that they argued much. I only saw them disagree about something a couple of times, or maybe that was because they mostly discussed stuff in private.'

'Were you an only child by choice?' Tillie asked.

'No.' He let out a sigh. 'Apparently my mother lost a baby—a little girl—seven months into the pregnancy when I was two. I don't remember anything about it, as I was too young.' A frown interrupted his features like a wind pattern on sand. 'My mother used to talk about her now and again. I realised later that would have been on my sister's birthday each year. She was called Lucy. After she lost her, Mum had to have a hysterectomy. I think it grieved her terribly. She was the sort of woman who would have loved a large family. But my dad used to always tell her he would rather have one child and her than to have more children and lose her. And then guess what happened.'

Tillie was glad he was talking more openly about his tragic background. It gave her the sense he was starting to trust her. That he was feeling close to her. Somehow that was important to her. They might be having a simple fling but it made her feel better to think he was not treating her as a come-and-go lover, but as someone he shared not just his body with but his thoughts and feelings and disappointments, too. In spite of his charming laugh-a-minute persona, she suspected he was quite a lonely man inside. Used to keeping his own counsel. Having to be strong for his father, to cope and shoulder far more responsibilities than he ought to have done. Had it isolated him? Made him lock down his emotions so no one got close enough to truly know and understand him?

'How did your dad deal with the loss of your sister?' she asked.

Blake examined the contents of his glass. 'A lot better than he handled Mum's death, that's for sure. He hasn't mentioned Lucy in years. But I guess it's different for expectant fathers. They aren't as closely bonded to the child as to the mother who's carrying it.'

'Maybe,' Tillie said and paused for a beat. 'You don't see yourself becoming a father one day? Even if you don't officially marry someone?'

He did a lip movement that was part-smile, part-grimace. 'It's not something I've thought about too much. I've had to concentrate on taking care of my father for so long I can't see myself signing up for more caretaking duties in a hurry.'

'You don't want an heir to inherit McClelland Park?'

'That's assuming I get it back. Nothing is certain yet.'

'But if you do,' Tillie said, 'wouldn't you want your own flesh and blood to carry on ownership rather than to have it sold to someone outside the McClelland family again?'

His expression lost some of its openness; it was as if shutters were being drawn down over a window. 'My goal is to get the Park back for my father. That's all I'm focussed on right now.'

Tillie could sense he wouldn't be pressed further on the subject. She wondered if his reasons for not settling down and having a family were because of his sad background or whether he truly didn't want to be tied down. A lot of modern men were fronting up later and later in life for fatherhood. But while men had the luxury to become fathers at just about any age, the issue was much more pressing for women. She didn't feel the pressure just yet, but she knew once she turned thirty it might be a different story. There had been a time when getting married and having a family were all she could think about. But now she wanted to concentrate on building up her business and getting her life back on track.

Blake pushed back from the table and began clearing the plates. 'Why don't you take Truffles out for a walk and I'll join you once I've cleared away here?'

Truffles sprang up from the floor and did a mad spin and gave a loud volley of barks as if to say, *Yes, please. Take me for a walk!*

The moon was a golden ball shining over the lake, a light breeze crinkling the surface of the water like wrinkles in a bolt of silk. An owl hooted and in the distance Tillie heard a vixen fox calling for a mate. Truffles had her nose to the ground and her tail in the air as she followed a scent in the garden and Tillie followed so as not to lose sight of her.

Within a few minutes, Tillie heard Blake's footsteps on the gravel pathway and then the softer tread of him moving across the damp velvet green lawn. She turned to look at him, her heart doing that funny tripping thing again. His shirt-sleeves were rolled back to his elbows from clearing away the dinner things, and his hair looked as if he had sent his hands through it for it looked more roughly tousled than it had earlier. He came to stand beside her, his shirtsleeve brushing her arm. It was barely touching her and yet it felt as if a strong fizzing current was being sent from his body to hers.

'So peaceful at this time of night,' he said, looking at the moonbeam shining over the lake.

'Yes… I'm going to find it hard to leave when the time comes,' Tillie said, and then wished she hadn't because of the passage of silence that ensued. Did he think she was fishing for an invitation to stay indefinitely? That she wanted their fling to go on and on?

But you do want it to go on.

She quickly barricaded the thought. She didn't want the same things as before. She was a changed woman. A single-and-loving-it woman. A woman who was embracing her passionate side without the restrictions of marriage and commitment. Their fling had just begun. They still had another few weeks to explore everything about each other. But once it was time to move on, she would move on as agreed.

Blake turned and looked down at her. 'What are your plans once you leave here?'

Tillie refused to acknowledge the twinge of disappointment his words evoked. She had no right to be disappointed he hadn't issued an invitation to stay on at the Park as long as she wanted.

'I haven't thought that far ahead,' she said. 'I only moved in here because Mr Pendleton's housekeeper retired just as he had his stroke and I had to move out of Simon's parents' cottage at short notice. It was never a long-term thing.'

'What will he do with Truffles if he moves into a care facility?'

Tillie glanced at the dog, who was busily chasing a moth. 'I don't know… I haven't discussed it with him. He loves that dog but I can't see him being able to take care of her properly now he's so frail.'

The dog came over to Blake and he leaned down to ruffle her ears. 'It must be hard growing old and losing control of all the things that are important to you,' he said.

'Terribly hard. I think that's why Mr Pendleton is so grumpy just now. He's struggling to come to terms with the limitations of aging.' Tillie rubbed at her upper arms to ward off a shiver from the cool breeze that had whipped up.

'Cold?' Blake asked, moving closer to put his arms around her.

'Warmer now.' She smiled at him. 'Much warmer.'

His eyes glinted in the moonlight. 'Let's get you inside where I can guarantee it's going to be hot.'

And it was.

Blake woke early the next morning and took Truffles for a long walk to allow Tillie time to get ready for work. He did a circuit of the lake and then went to the elm tree where he had carved his initials all those years ago. His fingers moved over the deeply grooved childish letters, remembering the heartache he'd felt as he'd carved them there. The heartache he still felt and would always feel until he could return this property to his father where it belonged.

The slight complication of where Tillie would live after he got the property back had kept him awake last night. He didn't want to turf her out on the streets or anything, but nor did he want to give her the impression this thing they had going could be anything more than it was. She kept insisting she was happy with a short-term fling. But where would she go after here? Her cake-decorating business was in the village, but there weren't many good quality rental opportunities available. He had already checked when he'd first come down to suss out the territory earlier that month. There was the bed and breakfast, but she wouldn't want to stay there unless she had the place to herself...

Blake let his mind run with the possibilities. When he'd checked out the other day, Maude Rosethorne had mentioned something in passing about retiring. The B&B would be a perfect set-up for Tillie to live and work from. The top floor could be her living space and the downstairs could be divided into kitchen and shop front with two rooms spare for a tearoom complete with cosy fireplaces. It was a perfect solution. What if he bought the B&B and gifted it to Tillie as a goodwill gesture? An end-of-the-affair thankyou gift?

Don't you mean a conscience-easing gift?

He wasn't listening to his conscience this time. This was about common sense. Sound business sense. Tillie would be able to expand her business and stay in the village where she was known and loved by everyone. She wouldn't have to worry about rent hikes and baking off site due to space issues.

Why hadn't he thought of it earlier? He would have to be careful how he broached the subject, however. She had a streak of stubborn pride he privately admired.

No, he would wait for a suitable opportunity to raise the topic with her and take things from there.

It being summer, Tillie had a rush of wedding cakes to see to at work. It meant her time with Blake over the next week or so was a little compromised, as she had to work at night on some of the more intricate decorations in between visiting Mr Pendleton as often as she could. It was frustrating because she knew her work time could be better managed if she had more revenue coming in, but her plan to relocate and expand her business to include a tearoom component had been shelved after she'd got into debt after her wedding was cancelled.

But rather than be put out by it, Blake simply took over things at the house. He had set up an office for himself where he conducted his business work, but he also spent time fixing things that were in need of a bit of maintenance in the house or on the property. When she came home each night after working, she found dinner cooked and ready to serve, and an exhausted Truffles, who had been exercised and fed and was usually lying on her back on her bed, with her head lolling to one side and with all four paws in the air in a state of complete and utter relaxation.

After her fourth and final day of working late, Tillie took the glass of wine Blake greeted her with and sank to the nearest chair and took three generous sips. 'You know, you'd make some lucky girl a wonderful husband one day. I mean, obviously not me since I'm not in the market for a husband, but someone. You cook, you clean, you're good with dogs and fixing broken stuff.'

Oops. Maybe I shouldn't drink on an empty stomach.

Blake's crooked smile didn't reach his eyes. 'Not going to happen.'

Tillie took a much more cautious sip of wine for something to do with her hands. 'I got rid of my wedding cake today.'

'You did?'

'Yeah. I'm quite proud of myself, actually.' She rose from her chair to fetch a glass of water. 'Next is my wedding dress. One of the brides who came in to order a cake today was interested. I might even make some money out of it. Who would've thought?'

When Tillie turned around from getting the water from the kitchen tap, he was leaning against the bench on the other side of the kitchen near the cooker, watching her steadily. She gave him an over-bright smile. 'Is something wrong?'

'What are your plans for your business?'

'Plans?'

'Do you have any expansion plans to increase your profit margin?'

Tillie put her water glass back down in the sink. 'You know, you really scare me sometimes with your mind-reading ability.'

'What would you like to do with the shop?'

Should she tell him of her hopes and dreams for her business? Why not? He was a smart businessman. Maybe he had some hints for her to make the most of her current position, limited as it was. 'I'd like it to be bigger for one thing. And I'd like to have a tearoom attached so that when people come in to order cakes they can also sit down and have lunch or high tea.'

'What's stopping you from acting on those plans?'

Tillie sighed. 'The M word.'

'Money?'

'Yup.'

'I could help you with that,' Blake said.

Tillie blinked. 'Pardon?'

He pushed himself away from the bench and came over to where she was standing. 'Maude Rosethorne wants to sell her B&B. I talked to her about it the other day. It would make a great venue for your shop.'

'I can't afford a place that size!' Tillie said. 'I'd never be able to manage the mortgage. I'm barely breaking even as it is.'

'I'm not talking about you taking out a mortgage.'

She licked her suddenly flour-dry lips. 'What are you talking about, then?'

His expression was as unreadable as the wall behind him. 'I would buy it for you.'

Tillie's mouth dropped open so far she thought she would crack a floorboard with her chin. 'You'd do...*what*?'

Still nothing showed on his face. If anything it became even more inscrutable as if every muscle had been snap frozen. 'It'd be a gift for—'

'For?' She leaned on the word, driving it home with a look.

'Tillie, think about it,' he said, some of the tightness of his face relaxing. Some. Not all. 'You're doing me a huge favour by helping me get back my family's home and I want to repay you.'

'No.' She moved to the other side of the room and folded her arms to glare at him. 'Seriously? What are people going to think?'

'They can think what they like,' he said. 'You don't have to tell them I bought it for you.'

Tillie gave a scornful laugh. 'I won't need to because Maude and her cronies will tell everyone for me. It'll be broadcast from every outpost. Everyone in the village will be talking about how you paid me off at the end of our affair like a mistress you want to keep sweet. No, thanks. I'll expand my business if and when I can do it under my own financial steam.' Even if the only financial steam she had going on right now was little more than a hiss.

Blake crossed the room to take her by the upper arms, his hands gently massaging the tension gathered there. 'Hey.'

Tillie pressed her lips together, shooting him a look from below her half-lowered lashes. 'And don't even think about buying me jewellery or a holiday house in the Bahamas, okay? That's even more tacky.'

His eyes were impossibly dark as they held hers, his body so close she could feel the electric pulse of it calling out to hers like a sonar signal. 'Is there anything you do want?'

I want you. She unwound her arms from across her middle and slid them up around his neck. 'Let's test that mind-reading ability of yours, shall we?'

A slow smile tipped up the sides of his mouth.

'You know that saying about getting out of the kitchen if you can't stand the heat?'

Tillie felt something unspool in her belly. 'I know it.'

He scooped her up and placed her on the bench, parting her thighs so he could stand between them. 'I'm about to turn the heat up. Think you can take it?'

'Try me.'

He brought his mouth down on hers in a blisteringly hot kiss that sent liquid heat to the core of her body. His hands tugged at her top, hauling it over her head before unclipping her bra and sending that to the floor as well. The rough urgency of his action thrilled her far more than the slow and tender sensuality of his previous lovemaking. His hands palpated her breasts and then he put his mouth to them in turn. His lips and tongue working their magic on her senses until she was whimpering and tearing at his clothes. Need surged in her body, raw, rampant need that wanted—begged for—immediate gratification.

His mouth closed over her nipple and areola; drawing on her in a sucking motion that was part pleasure, part pain. He went to her other breast, subjecting it to the same delicious attention before he came back up to her mouth. His tongue met hers in a stabbing thrust, duelling with it, mating with it in a dance that had echoes of lust in every pulse-racing second.

Tillie got working on the fastener on his waistband, releasing the zip so she could take him in her hands. He lifted up her skirt and pushed her knickers aside to touch her intimately. She was so worked up she almost came on the spot, her body wet and hungry, empty and aching for the pressure and friction of his.

He pulled her down off the bench and turned her so she had her back to him. She braced herself by gripping the edge of the bench while he sourced a condom, every cell of her body throbbing with excitement in the countdown to intimate contact.

He drove in from behind, the slick force of him snatching her breath and sending a hot shiver coursing down the back of her legs in quicksilver streaks. His movements increased in urgency but she was with him all the way, the almost shockingly primitive rhythm speaking to her flesh in a way she hadn't thought possible. The orgasm came with such force it made her bite back a scream as the sensations catapulted her into a spinning vortex. The spasms went on and on, deeper, richer, spreading to every corner and crevice of her body in ever increasing waves like a large stone dropped in a pond. Even her skin felt as if it had been electrified with a thousand tiny electrodes, raising it in a shower of goose bumps.

Blake gave a deep, shuddering groan and emptied, his hands gripping her hips until she was sure she would find a full set of his fingerprints on her flesh. He relaxed his hold once the storm had passed, his hands turning her so she was facing him. He was still breathing heavily, his eyes sexily bright with the gleam of satisfaction. 'You never cease to excite me.'

Tillie toyed with one of his dark curls of hair at the back of his neck. 'You do a pretty good job of exciting me, too.'

He brushed her mouth with his. 'Are you ready for dinner or do you have something you have to do first?'

'Only this,' she said and brought his mouth back down to hers.

Blake wasn't sure what woke him later that night. He glanced at Tillie lying beside him but she was fast asleep, one of her hands resting on his chest, her head buried against his neck. He'd been dreaming and then he'd woken with a jolt but he couldn't remember what the dream contained. All he had was a vague feeling of unease, as if a centuries-old ghost had stepped out of the ancient woodwork and placed a cold hand on the back of his neck.

The old house creaked around him, the noises both familiar and strange.

Or maybe it was his lingering sense of frustration Tillie hadn't accepted his offer of the B&B premises that was disturbing his sleep. He'd already spoken to Maude Rosethorne about buying it—thankfully he hadn't said who or what for. He'd simply made her an offer and left her to think about it. But it wouldn't take much for Maude to join the dots once the time came for his fling with Tillie to end.

What was Tillie's problem? It was a generous gesture on his part and there were no strings attached. It was a gift that would keep on giving. Why wouldn't she accept it and leave it at that?

He glanced at her again, his hand moving to brush a wisp of hair away from her mouth. She gave a soft murmur and brushed at her face with her hand as if shooing away whatever had tickled her face.

He'd spent the whole night with lovers before. Lots of times. He wasn't that cold and clinical about the boundaries of a fling that he couldn't bring himself to share a bed with a sexual partner. But no one he'd shared a bed with had made him want to hold them close all night and every night. Usually, the longer the affair continued, so the distance between them in the bed increased. It was the subtle way he sent the signal that their time was coming to a close.

But somehow with Tillie he was moving closer, not further apart. He would wake to find himself spooning with her, or with her legs entwined with his and her head resting on his chest, his arms wrapped around her. Whenever she moved away he felt a strange sense of disquiet…as if something was missing.

Tillie suddenly opened her eyes and shifted against him like a warm kitten wanting to be stroked. 'What time is it?' Her voice had a sleepy huskiness to it that sent his blood south of the border.

'Too early to get up.'

Her hand slipped down from his chest to his groin. 'Looks like you're already up,' she said with a little smile that curled the edges of her mouth.

'I've used my last condom,' he said. 'I meant to pick some up on my way home but forgot.' How had he got through so many in the last week? Normally he had plenty to spare at this stage of a fling.

'We could do it without,' she said. 'I'm on the pill and we're exclusive…aren't we? And we're both free of any nasty diseases.'

Blake had seen her packet of contraceptive pills in the bathroom cupboard. He'd felt a bit of a jerk checking each day to see if she'd taken it, but still. He had to be sure she was being honest with him over what she wanted. But a part of him was worried she was in denial. She'd been hurt by the jilting. Deeply hurt. Who wouldn't be? It was the ultimate in rejection to be dumped on the day of the wedding you had planned and looked forward to for months.

But what if she was only saying what she thought he wanted to hear? What if behind her I'm-cool-with-the-terms-of-our-fling attitude was a secret yearning for it to morph into something else?

Something more lasting…

A frown suddenly interrupted her features. 'Why are you looking at me like that?'

Blake toned down the frown he hadn't realised had formed on his forehead. 'How am I looking at you?'

'Like you're cross with me or something.'

He stretched his mouth into a smile and tucked a strand of hair behind her ear. 'I'm not cross with you. Far from it.'

She chewed her lower lip as if she was mulling over something. 'Have you ever done it without a condom?'

'No.'

'Not ever?'

'No,' he said. 'Too much of a control freak.'

She began to trace a pathway over his clavicle with her fingertip, her eyes watching the passage of her finger instead of meeting his. 'If you don't want to, then that's fine. We can wait until tomorrow.'

Blake did want to. He wanted to so badly it wouldn't have mattered if some of those little pills hadn't been taken. If *none* of those pills had been taken. Right now he needed her as he had needed no one before. It was a fire in his blood. A red-hot fever that could not be quelled. He rolled her so she was beneath him and she gave a little gasp of surprise when his erection bumped against her mound. 'Sorry. Am I rushing you?' he said, checking himself.

Her hands grabbed him by the buttocks, drawing him close to her damp heat. 'I want you.'

'I want you too, so much,' he said, sinking in between her silken wet folds with a groan.

I can't seem to stop wanting you.

Her legs wrapped around his and he rocked with her in a frenzied quest for satiation. His skin was alive with nerve endings, his blood racing, pounding with the thrill of being as close as it was possible to be to another person. Not just skin on skin. Intimate skin on skin. His mouth fed off hers, his tongue tangling erotically with hers, escalating the pulse of lust driving through him. He reached between their striving bodies, his fingers finding her swollen flesh, and within seconds she erupted into a rippling orgasm that catapulted him into the abyss...

Blake lost track of time. It could have been seconds, minutes or even half an hour before either of them spoke. He stroked the back of her head where her hair was matted from rubbing against the pillow. He was still a little stunned by the sensations that powered through him. Making love with her seemed to get better and better. More satisfying. More exciting.

More...everything.

Her fingers did a soft tiptoeing thing against his sternum. 'Blake?'

'Mmm?'

'It was a nice thought about buying Maude's B&B,' she said. 'A really nice thought.'

'But you won't accept it from me.' He didn't frame it as a question but as a matter of fact.

She raised her gaze to his. 'I've already accepted way too much off you. The money you paid off my debts with. This ridiculously expensive ring I'm wearing.'

He stroked a fingertip over the small frown

creasing her forehead. 'I don't want you to feel exploited when this is over.'

Her eyes slipped out of reach of his. 'What if Mr Pendleton takes longer than you expected to make up his mind about selling? What if *this*—' she emphasised the word slightly '—drags on for longer than you expected?'

Blake was well aware things weren't going strictly according to plan. The old man was proving tricky to win over. He'd been sure the announcement of his engagement to Tillie would be enough to seal the deal but, if anything, it had complicated things. Deeply complicated things. Close to two weeks had already gone by and the old codger hadn't budged. Another week or two might improve negotiations, but it would also further cement the bond that was developing between Blake and Tillie. A bond he normally didn't form with anyone during a fling. The sort of bond that would not be so easy to dismantle when it was time to move on. Not just a bond of friendship and mutual admiration, but an intimate connection he had never felt with anyone before now.

He felt her touch in places no one had ever reached. It was as if she reached right into his chest with her soft dainty hand, resting it against the membrane of his heart. He could feel it right now. A presence. A weight. A pressure. Every time he breathed it was like he was breathing with her.

'We'll see how the rest of the month pans out and then we'll take stock,' he said. 'That is, unless you're getting bored already?'

She gave a soft laugh and snuggled closer. 'Not yet, but I'll let you know.'

CHAPTER NINE

TILLIE WAS SERVING one of her regular customers in the shop when Simon's mother, Marilyn, came in. She kept her professional and polite smile in place and made sure her engagement ring was clearly on show when she placed her hands on top of the counter.

'Hello, Marilyn, what can I do for you today?'

'I'm not here to buy anything,' Marilyn said. 'I just wanted to…to see how you are.'

'Well, as you can see, I'm just fine,' Tillie said. 'But it was nice of you to think of me and take time out of your busy day to drop by.'

When you haven't graced me with your obnoxious presence for nearly four months.

Marilyn gave a version of a smile—a movement of her lips that looked like a thin ribbon stretching. 'Have you been in contact with Simon? I mean, recently?'

'No. No contact. But it's better that way, especially now I'm engaged and—'

'It was wrong what he did to you, Tillie,' Marilyn said, her hands gripping her handbag against her stomach. 'Terribly, unforgivably wrong. I should have said something before now. But the thing is… I always felt he was wrong for you. That's why I didn't encourage the relationship. I must have hurt you by being so cold and distant, but I thought you would finally realise you could do much better than Simon.'

Much better than her precious perfect son?

Tillie wasn't sure she was hearing properly. Could this confession/apology be for real? 'Look, it's really nice of you to—'

'I'm glad you've found someone,' Marilyn said. 'From all I've heard so far, Blake McClelland seems perfect husband material and apparently madly in love with you. I'm pleased for you, dear. I was worried you'd end up alone and moping about Simon for the rest of your life.'

Not flipping likely.

Tillie hadn't thought about Simon in weeks. She could barely recall what he looked like. 'Blake is a wonderful man and I'm very lucky he came along when he did.'

And isn't that the truth?

Her life was completely different now Blake was a part of it. She smiled more, she laughed more. She felt more. Things she had never felt before. Not just sexual things but other things.

Things that could not be so easily described.

Marilyn's expression turned sour. 'When I think of how I could have had you as a daughter-in-law instead of…of that…that creature Simon met online. And now he's gone and got her pregnant so there'll be no getting rid of her now. She'll want a ring on her finger and a big flashy wedding.'

Tillie expected to feel shocked, even a little sad at the news of Simon becoming a father, but instead she felt…nothing. It was as if Marilyn were talking about a stranger. Someone who had not been in her life at all. 'But it will be nice for you to have a grandchild, won't it?'

Marilyn's eyes looked suspiciously moist. 'Oh, Tillie, how can you be so…so nice about this? I know your dad and stepmother brought you up to be polite and gracious but surely it's not healthy to be so calm and accepting about this? If you weren't so happy with Blake I would beg you to come back and talk some sense into Simon. But I guess that's not possible, is it?'

Tillie's conscience gave her a tiny prod. She was far too happy with Blake. Dangerously happy. What-am-I-going-to-do-now? happy. 'No. It's not.'

Soon after Marilyn left, Tillie saw an email had finally come in from her father and stepmother. She opened the message to find their monthly newsletter they sent to all their friends with a short missive addressed to her at the bottom, briefly congratulating her on her engagement and expressing their pleasure in her ability to forgive and move on from Simon.

She stared at the message for a long moment. So the main issue for them was still her forgiving Simon. Didn't they want to know more about Blake? How happy he made her? How much he made her feel alive? Didn't they want to rush home to meet him? Wasn't her happiness more important to them than anything else? She knew the problems her father and stepmother dealt with in Uganda were not trivial. They were life and death issues and she had no business feeling piqued they hadn't shown more interest in what was happening in her life. But just like the time they had moved parishes, she was left standing on the station platform, feeling terribly alone.

Later that day, Tillie went with Truffles to see Mr Pendleton after work. Blake had texted her to tell her he had some business to see to and would see her at home later, promising to take her out to dinner to save her from cooking.

Mr Pendleton was sitting in a recliner chair in his room and looking listlessly out of the window, but immediately brightened when she came in with Truffles. 'Ah, my two favourite girls.' He fondled the dog's ears and then looked at Tillie. 'Well, well, well, you've certainly got a glow about you these days.'

The only glow Tillie was aware of was the one currently blazing from her cheeks. Could Mr Pendleton somehow see that only that morning she'd had smoking-hot sex with Blake in the shower and all these hours later her body was still tingling? 'Have I?'

'So the engagement is still going strong, then, is it?'

'Yes. We're very happy. He's fun to be around and he's wonderful with Truffles. He takes her for long walks and he clears away after dinner. And he's sorted out a few maintenance issues at the Park for you. What's not to love?'

His expression was suddenly like an inquisitive bird. 'So you actually...*love* him?'

'Of course I love him,' Tillie said.

Gosh, how easy is this lying caper getting? That didn't even feel like a lie.

It had felt so easy to say much the same to Simon's mother earlier that day. She hadn't felt as if she was lying at all. The words had tripped off her tongue with an authenticity she couldn't explain. Didn't want to explain.

'Maybe I was wrong about that man,' he said. 'It's not that I don't like him. I do. He's got backbone, drive, ambition.'

I like him, too. Maybe a little too much.

Tillie sat down on the visitor's chair next to his chair. 'Have you decided what you're going to do about McClelland Park?'

Mr Pendleton's eyes met hers in a searching manner. 'Is that what you want, Tillie? To live there with him and raise the family you've always wanted?'

Tillie's throat was suddenly blocked as if she had tried to swallow one of the pillows.

Oh, God. Oh, God. Oh, God.

Why hadn't she realised this until now? Or had she done her usual thing of ignoring the blatantly obvious? Living in a state of denial until it was too late. No wonder she hadn't been upset to hear about her ex becoming a father, because the only person she wanted to father her children was Blake. The man she had fallen hopelessly in love with in spite of every promise and assurance not to. How could she not fall in love with him? He was everything she longed for in a partner.

He wasn't just Mr Right.

He was Mr Perfect.

He was *her* person. The go-to person she could talk to about stuff she hadn't talked about with anyone else. The person who listened and felt things on her behalf and made her feel things she had never felt before.

'Yes,' she said. 'I want that more than anything.'

It wasn't a lie. It was true. In every way it could be it was true. She wanted to be with Blake. Not just in a short-term fling.

She wanted to stay with him for ever.

Who was she kidding? She wasn't a single-and-loving-it girl. She was a marriage-or-nothing girl. It wasn't something she could change on a whim like changing a pair of shoes.

It wasn't changeable.

It was indelibly printed on her soul—she was a girl who wanted the fairy tale because she knew she couldn't be happy with anyone other than Blake. She didn't have to have heaps of flings with a bunch of men to know he was the right man for her.

The *only* man for her.

As soon as he'd kissed her something had happened that had ruined her for anyone else. He had turned on her passion—passion that could only ever be triggered by him.

Mr Pendleton released a sigh. 'I might be an old man now but I still remember what it was like to be in love. I miss my Velma every day.'

'I know, it must be so lonely for you.'

He tapped his gnarled fingers on the arms of his chair, his caterpillar-like brows almost touching over his eyes. 'I'm going to have to do something about that dog. I can't take her where I'm going.'

Tillie swallowed again. 'Where do you plan to go?'

'Plan?' He made a scoffing noise. 'That's the damn trouble with getting old. You lose the ability to plan anything. Things happen and you have no control over them.'

'It must be very hard…'

He turned his head to look out of the window again, blinking a couple of times in rapid succession, and his dentures making a clicking noise as if he was swallowing against a tide of emotion. Truffles stopped chewing the rubber doorstop behind the door and came over and sat with her head on his knee and gave him a melting look. His hand absently stroked her head and he slowly turned to look at Tillie. 'I'm going to move into a care facility. I don't want to but I can't manage on my own. The Park's way too big for an old man like me. The place is meant to be for a family, not some old geezer with one and a half feet in the grave.'

Tillie grasped one of his hands, so close to tears she could feel them stinging her eyes. 'I'll still come and visit you every day. And I'll take care of Truffles and bring her in with me—that is, if they allow dogs to visit.'

His expression had a touch of wryness about it. 'Won't you be too busy making babies to be worrying about me?'

No, I won't. I'll be sitting on my own watching PG movies with a dog chewing anything that isn't nailed down.

Blake swung by the respite facility on his way home to see Mr Pendleton before he took Tillie out to dinner. The old man had left a message on his phone saying he wanted to speak to him. He tried not to get too excited. Mr Pendleton could be manipulating him for all he knew. The month was almost up. He would have to make a decision soon for he couldn't stay in respite indefinitely. He would have to be moved to somewhere where his needs could be taken care of going forward. Blake wasn't going to get his hopes too high until he had seen the old man's signature on the documents.

He had a special evening planned for Tillie.

Dinner in a small but excellent restaurant he'd got to hear of via a business client. After dinner there was a wine bar with live music for dancing, and after that home to bed.

Home.

It was funny how he was starting to think of McClelland Park and Tillie as if they were inextricably linked. But in a way they were. She was the reason he was this close to getting his ancestral home back. If he pulled this off, he would always be grateful for her role in that.

But it was more than that. Tillie made the big old house feel like a home. All the little touches she gave that reminded him of his mother. The vases of fragrant flowers, the home-baked goodies stacked in tins in the pantry, the freshly aired rooms and crisp clean linen on the bed. The house had a vibrant, almost palpable energy in it when she was there. On the days he'd got home first, the house had seemed cavernous, cold, creaky. But Tillie's bright presence shone light into every dark corner of that house.

Mr Pendleton was sitting by the window in a recliner chair and for a moment Blake stood watching from the doorway. The old man looked sad and weary, his thin frame seeming shrunken, as if the bones of his skeleton were too tired to hold him upright.

'Jim?'

The old man turned his head to look at him. 'McClelland.'

Blake brought another chair closer, his nostrils picking up a faint trace of Tillie's perfume in the air. 'Has Tillie just been in?'

'Half an hour ago,' Mr Pendleton said. 'She brought the dog. She's going to keep her for me. I can't take her into the care facility with me.'

'That's a shame,' Blake said. 'But Tillie will do an awesome job of looking after Truffles.'

Mr Pendleton's birdlike gaze pecked at his. 'She tells me she's in love with you. I didn't believe it the first time she told me. But I do now.'

Blake ignored the faint prickle on his scalp. Tillie was a fine actor. She knew how much he wanted to buy the Park back. She was pulling all the stops out to help him. Of course she was acting like a woman in love because that was their agreement. He was doing a damn fine impression of a man in love, too. Damn fine.

'I'm a lucky man,' he said, throwing in a smile for good measure.

Mr Pendleton's expression looked like a scrunched-up paper bag. 'You don't fool me for a second, McClelland. You're not in love with her.'

Maybe his acting could do with a little work after all.

'What makes you think that?'

'How far will you go to get back McClelland Park?'

Blake resisted the urge to shift his weight under the piercing scrutiny of the old man's gaze. He'd tussled and won with much tougher old men than Jim Pendleton. Much tougher. 'I'm prepared to pay you more than the market price. Double, even.'

Mr Pendleton gave a breath of a laugh. 'Money. You think I want money at this time of life? What I need is…never mind what I need.' His brows drew together again. 'I'll sell you the place. I was always going to, you know.'

You were?

Blake was proud of his poker face. So why the run around? What had the old man hoped to achieve? A last ditch at power games? He didn't know whether to be relieved his goal was finally nailed or angry he'd been made to jump through hoops like a circus dog.

'I loved living there all these years but it's never been the same without Velma and my daughter, Alice,' Mr Pendleton said. 'That's what makes a place a home—the people who live in it with you. But you don't need me to tell you that. I'm sure you remember all too well how empty a place can be once you lose someone you love.'

That was why Blake didn't love anyone *that* much. Not enough to be devastated when they were no longer there. Not enough to wrench his heart out of his chest and leave a giant bleeding, gaping hole.

'When do you want me to draw up the paperwork?' he said.

'As soon as you like,' Mr Pendleton said.

Blake wondered why he wasn't feeling the sense of satisfaction he'd thought he'd be feeling right now. He'd done it. He'd got the old man to agree to sell him back his home. 'Would you like me to take you to the Park so Tillie and I can help you sort through your things?'

Mr Pendleton shook his head. 'I couldn't bear it. I hate goodbyes.'

Yes, well, I'm not so fond of them, either.

Tillie was in the sitting room pacing the floor when Blake came in and dropped a kiss on her mouth before she could even say hello. 'Hey, guess what?' he said. 'Jim's agreed to sell me the Park.'

She knew she should be feeling happy for him but instead she felt sad. This was it. The end of the affair. 'You must be thrilled.'

He frowned at her listless tone. 'What's wrong? We did it. You did it, actually.' He gave a light chuckle. 'You totally convinced the old man you were in love with me.'

There was a beat of silence.

'That's because I am in love with you.'

His expression flinched as if she'd slapped him. He stepped further away as if distancing himself from such raw emotion. 'You don't mean that.' His voice had a rough edge to it. Harsh almost.

Tillie had been expecting exactly this reaction but, even so, a frail hope had still managed to rise in her chest that he might feel the same way about her. 'I do mean it, Blake. I know it's not what you want to hear but I can't help it. I had to tell you.'

'Don't do this, Tillie.'

'What am I doing?' she said. 'You said I could call it off when it was time. Well, it's time. You've got what you wanted. You've got back McClelland Park.'

His jaw worked for a moment as if he were trying to avoid swallowing a marble. 'Yes, but that doesn't mean we have to end things right here and now.'

'Then when will we end it? A week from now? A month? Two months?'

'As long as we're happy with how things are going—'

'But I'm not happy,' Tillie said. 'I'm playing

a role I wasn't cut out for. I might be good at it but it's not true to who I am. I want more than great sex. I want marriage and commitment and kids and—'

'Hold on a minute.' He held up a hand. 'You told me you weren't interested in any of that stuff any more. You said you were against marriage. You said no man would ever get you to wear a white dress and show up at church. Those were your exact words or close to them.'

Tillie let out a shaky breath. 'I know I said that. And I meant it at the time but—'

'Yeah, well, I meant what I said back then and I still mean it,' he said. 'I'm not interested in marrying you or anyone. I was completely honest with you on that and now you tell me you want me to change? Well, guess what, sweetheart. Not going to happen.' He strode to the other side of the room, standing in front of the fireplace with his hands gripping the mantelpiece so tightly as if he was going to tear it from its moorings.

Tillie had thought reading that text from Simon was bad but this was something else again. Her heart felt as if it were being crushed until she could barely draw in a breath. Her throat was knotted with emotion. 'Did these last weeks mean anything to you? Anything at all?'

He swung back around to glare at her. 'What's

happened from this morning in the shower to now? I seem to remember you were pretty happy about the terms of our fling then.'

Tillie momentarily closed her eyes so she didn't have to see the acrid bitterness of his gaze. But when she opened them he had turned his back on her and was leaning against the mantelpiece again.

'Three things,' she said. 'I got a visit from Simon's mother this morning.' She saw the muscles of his back and shoulders stiffen. 'He and his partner are having a baby.'

Blake turned back to face her, his expression guarded. 'Were you upset?'

'No, not as much as I thought I would be, or should be,' Tillie said. 'But it made me realise I do want a family. Not just a kid with some random guy but with—'

'No. No. No.' His words were like a nail gun firing into a slab of timber.

'Blake, at least hear me out,' she said. 'I haven't told you about the second and third things.'

'Go on.' His lips barely moved as he spoke and he had his granite face back on.

She took another breath. 'My parents finally emailed me. They congratulated me on my engagement but I couldn't help feeling it was my being able to forgive Simon that was their main concern. Not whether I was happy and fulfilled but as long as I had done the right thing by Simon.'

'You can't change people so don't bother—'

'I'm not interested in changing my parents,' Tillie said. 'Anyway, I'm the one who's changed. I know what I want now and I'm not afraid of asking for it. You're the one who taught me that, Blake.'

His expression was still so stony it could have doubled for a retaining wall. 'You mentioned a third thing.'

'The third thing is I went to see Mr Pendleton after work. He asked me what I wanted. Whether I wanted to live here with you and make babies and I realised that's exactly what I want. I want that more than anything.'

He closed his eyes, as if hoping she wouldn't be standing there saying such things when he opened them again. 'I'm sorry, Tillie. But I can't give you the fairy tale. I told you that right from the start. I'm not—'

'I know, I know, I know,' she said. 'You're not the settling-down type. Well, here's the thing. I am. Which means we are at an impasse.'

He rubbed at his face as if he could erase the last few minutes. 'So you're ending our fling.'

'That was the plan, wasn't it? That I would be the one to call time?'

He gave a laugh that was a long way from amusement. 'Your timing sure could do with some work.'

So could your attitude.

'What? You wanted me to go out and celebrate with you on successfully achieving your goal?' Tillie asked. 'I can't do that, Blake. I won't do it. I've felt compromised the whole time we've run with this charade. I never wanted it in the first place. You forced it on me with your...your damned generosity, which isn't really generosity because you're so rich you probably don't even notice the dip in your bank account.'

'I'm not going to stand here and apologise for being successful.'

'You might be successful in terms of money and business but you're not successful where it counts,' she said. 'You've got this house back. Well done. But what about when you're Mr Pendleton's age? What then? Who is going to be there for you? Or will you have to pay someone or blackmail someone?'

A muscle beat a pulse in his face like a tiny fist punching its way through his cheek. His eyes were so smoky and grey they looked like brooding storm clouds. 'I think you've made your position clear. Do you want me to help you pack or have you already done so?'

How could he be so cruel? So cold and unfeeling? As if she were a guest who had outstayed her welcome. But maybe that was exactly what she was. A visitor in his life. A passing fancy he had indulged in to achieve a goal but now he was done with her. He didn't need her. He didn't want her.

He didn't love her.

'I'll go and do it now,' Tillie said without showing any of the emotion that was climbing up her throat. Pride had got her into this mess and pride would get her out of it. 'But you'll have to mind Truffles because I can't take her to a hotel. Once I sort out some accommodation I'll make arrangements to come and get her.'

'Fine.'

Blake took the dog for a walk so he didn't have to see Tillie leaving. Why did she have to choose today to end their fling? He was supposed to be celebrating the successful buy-back of his home and now she'd ruined it by insisting they end their affair. That it was almost time on the month they'd agreed on wasn't the issue. It was the fact she'd dropped that I-love-you-and-want-to-have-babies-with-you bomb. He couldn't have made it clearer to her he wasn't the poster boy for marriage. He had made no promises, given her no false leads, told no lies. He'd been brutally hon-

est and now she was telling him she wanted him
to be the prince in her fairy tale.

But the main thing was he had McClelland
Park back. That was what he should be focussing
on, not the fact Tillie had called time.

Truffles pricked up her ears at the sound of Tillie's car moving down the ribbon of the driveway
and she whined and cocked her head from side to
side as if in confusion. Blake reached down and
held her collar just in case she took chase. 'She'll
be back for you, Truffles.'

The dog strained against his hold and whined
again, every muscle in her body poised to spring
off in pursuit.

'Yeah, I know the feeling,' Blake said. 'But
believe me, you'll get over it.'

CHAPTER TEN

TILLIE HAD THOUGHT facing everybody after she'd been jilted had been tough, but when news got out her engagement to Blake was over she was besieged by disappointment from everyone in the village. It was brilliant for business as people came into the shop on the pretext of buying cakes, and, once they had their goodies bought and packaged, they would offer a word or two—or a few lengthy paragraphs—on why they were so devastated on her behalf as they thought Blake was perfect for her. Her profits shot up and she had to do extra time in the kitchen to keep up. She had even managed to attract a growing celebrate-a-break-up clientele. Tragic that somehow she was the poster girl for broken relationships, but she embraced it and added a new page to her website.

Tillie had managed to secure a pet-friendly rental property in the village and Blake had dropped the dog off while Tillie was at work. The fact he hadn't waited till she got home was both a relief and a bitter disappointment. So he didn't want to see her? Fine. She didn't want to scc him, either.

The house she was renting was more of a housesitting arrangement but that suited her, as she wanted some time to think about what she would do next. She didn't want to pack up and leave the village, but if this intense focus on her love life, or lack thereof, continued she would go send-for-a-straitjacket mad.

Mr Pendleton had moved into the care facility, and, while it was a nice place with lovely staff—most of whom he knew in one way or the other—Tillie was conscious it was not home for him. How could it be? He couldn't have Truffles there and he seemed a little more dejected each day she visited.

McClelland Park had been signed over to Blake but that was all she'd heard or seen of him since he'd texted to say he'd dropped off Truffles.

Joanne was the only one who didn't commiserate with her. 'I think you should have stuck with him until he realised he was in love with you,' she said.

'But he's not in love with me,' Tillie said, putting the last touches on a divorce party cake.

Never was.

Never will be.

'Then why has he not been seen out with anyone else since your break-up?' Joanne pointed at the effigy of the ex on the top of the cake they were decorating. 'This guy's been seen out with four women since he separated from Gina. Bastard.'

Tillie drove a metal skewer through the groin of the marzipan figure. 'There. That should slow him down at bit.'

'Why haven't you made a break-up cake for yourself?' Joanne asked after a moment. 'We could have a party. I'll help you with the catering. You don't have to pay me. I'll do it for free.'

Tillie stood back from her handiwork. 'I don't need to get Blake McClelland out of my system. I'm over him.'

Not quite true. She spent most nights tossing in bed feeling empty and hollow. Her body missed him in every cell and pore. She sometimes felt she could still feel him moving inside her but then she would wake from that dream and realise with a sinking feeling he wasn't in the bed beside her. His arms weren't wrapped around her; his chin wasn't resting on the top of her head.

She was alone.

'Then why are you still wearing his ring?'

Tillie looked down at the diamond on her hand. For some reason, in spite of the weight she'd lost over the last two weeks, it was still firmly lodged on her finger. 'I haven't had time to have it cut off, that's why. But as soon as I get it off I'm going to give it back to him.'

Blake called on his father the day McClelland Park was officially signed over to him. He figured the last two weeks of misery he'd gone through would be worth it to see his dad's face when he presented the deeds to the house to him. Misery he hadn't expected to feel—misery that had eaten at his guts until he could barely take in food or water.

He didn't understand what was wrong with him. He'd been the one to draw up the month-long plan with Tillie. Surely by now he should be feeling it was worth it.

'Dad, I want you to come with me for the weekend. I have a surprise for you.'

Andrew McClelland looked faintly sheepish. 'Now's not a good time for me. I have…something on this weekend.'

Blake frowned. 'Since when have you had something on a weekend? Every time I come here you're sitting staring blankly at the walls.'

His dad kept holding the front door of his town

house in London only slightly ajar as if he was hiding something. 'Can we make it another time?'

Maybe his dad was doing his sad recluse thing, where he would lock the doors and close the blinds and not see or speak to anyone for days. Blake glanced at the window where his father's bedroom was situated. Yep, blinds down. 'Come on, Dad. I've been planning this for weeks. Surely nothing you're doing is that important. Some fresh air and sunshine will do you good.'

'I have someone with me just now.'

Someone? What someone? Blake frowned so hard he could have cracked a walnut between his brows. 'What's going on?'

His dad's cheeks had more colour in them than Blake had seen in years. 'I'm entertaining a guest.'

His dad was entertaining a guest? The man who had lived alone and refused to even go out shopping was *entertaining* someone? The man who consistently refused to come to any of the dinners and bridge parties and gatherings Blake organised for him in order to get him socialising a bit more actually had someone over? 'Who?'

'A lady I met at the heart rehab centre,' his father said. 'A widow. She lost her husband when she was in her thirties and hasn't been out with anyone since. We've struck up a friendship, well, more than a friendship. Can you come back some other time?'

Great. His dad was now officially having more sex than he was. Not that Blake wanted to have sex with anyone. Not since Tillie had ended their fling. Sex with someone else was the last thing on his mind. He got sick to the stomach thinking about getting it on with someone else. He couldn't imagine kissing or touching them the way he longed to be touching Tillie.

'I was going to tell you but you've been so preoccupied lately,' his dad said.

Preoccupied? I guess you could call it that.

'Dad, I bought back McClelland Park,' Blake said. 'I've been working on it for the last month. You have your home back. You can go back and live there any time you like. It's yours. I have the deeds here and—'

'Oh, Blake, I don't know what to say...' His dad's expression clouded. 'It's a wonderful gesture. Truly wonderful and typical of you to always think of me. But I can't go back.'

Can't go back?

What did he mean, he couldn't go back? Blake had turned inside out and back to front to get that damn property back. How could his dad not want to live there? 'But you love that place,' Blake said.

'It's your home. The place where you were the happiest and where—'

'It ceased to be home once your mum died,' his dad said. 'That part of my life is over. I'm finally moving on. If I were to go and live there now it would be like going backwards. I loved everything about that place, but without your mother it's nothing to me. It's just a big old empty house.'

'But it wouldn't be empty if you lived there with your new lady friend,' Blake said. 'You could set up a nice home together and—'

'I could, but that would be doing what you think is best for me instead of what *I* think is best for me,' his dad said. 'I know it's been tough on you these last twenty-four years. I've been a terrible burden on you and I want that to stop. Right here. Right now.'

Blake swallowed back his disappointment but it stuck in his throat like a tyre jack. His father didn't want McClelland Park? He had worked so hard to get that place back…for…for *nothing*? He had compromised himself. Stepped over personal boundaries, got caught up in a relationship with Tillie that he should be well and truly over by now.

'Blake, please,' his dad said. 'Will you just go? I'm okay. You don't have to babysit me any more. I'll call you in a day or two and Susie and I will have you over to dinner. You can bring someone if you like. Are you seeing anyone at the moment?'

So now his dad was organising Blake's social life for him? Weird. Just so damn weird. 'No one special.'

'Oh, well, just come on your own, then,' his dad said. 'We won't mind.'

No. But I will.

Tillie could see storm clouds brewing all Friday afternoon when she was working on the last touches of a cake for a client for a wedding on the Saturday. The power had threatened to go off a couple of times and she couldn't stop thinking about Truffles back at the cottage she was house-sitting. Truffles hated storms. She hid under furniture or cowered in corners and whimpered as if the end of the world were at hand. It was distressing enough to watch, but not being there to make sure the poor dog was all right was a different type of torture altogether.

Tillie rushed back to the cottage early, leaving Joanne to close up the shop. The wind was howling and whipping the branches of the trees along the street as she approached. But when she arrived outside the cottage her heart came to a juddering halt. The gate leading to the front path was not just open but hanging off its hinges and a limb of one of the ornamental trees was lying across the pathway. Doing her best to shelter from the wind-driven pellets of rain and hail, Tillie dashed around to the back garden but there was no sign of the dog.

Panic beat a tattoo in her chest that was even louder than the hail falling on the cobblestone path. The one thing Mr Pendleton looked forward to each day was seeing Truffles. How could Tillie tell him she had lost her? What if Truffles was hit by a car and lying bleeding and broken in some rain-soaked and debris-ridden gutter? What if the dog was critically injured and had gone out of sight to die in one of the nearby hedgerows or fields or woods? It would break Mr Pendleton's heart if he lost Truffles. It would make him ever more despondent and depressed, and no amount of Tillie's marshmallow slice would cheer him up.

Tillie ran up and down the street calling for the dog but all she got for her effort was sodden with rain and splashed with mud. Her stomach was churning with dread—a cold fist that clutched at her insides until she had to stop and bend over with her hands resting on her knees to draw breath.

How could this be happening?

Where would Truffles have gone?

Think. Think. Think.

Could Truffles have headed to McClelland Park? It was her home after all, the place where she had spent the first two years of her life. The cottage here was not as familiar to her and perhaps she got spooked while out in the garden and took off.

Tillie didn't stop to consider the possibility of running into Blake. As far as she knew he hadn't been back to the Park since the sale was finalised. It wouldn't take her long to have a quick look around and see if Truffles had headed there. It was a few kilometres away, but she knew dogs could travel much further than that when distressed.

Please be there. Please be there. Please be there.

But Tillie wasn't sure if she was praying about the dog or Blake or both.

Blake decided to go down to McClelland Park for the weekend in any case. So what if his father was too busy with his new love-nest buddy to celebrate the return of their ancestral home with him? So what if the weather turned foul as if to add a further insult? It could rain and hail on his parade for all it liked. He did not give a damn. He would drink the champagne and eat the caviar by himself. He had a right to celebrate, didn't he?

He had achieved what he'd set out to achieve. So what if his father didn't want to live there now? It didn't matter. The place was back in McClelland hands and that was where it would stay.

Living there himself hadn't really crossed Blake's mind...well, maybe that wasn't strictly true. It had crossed his mind. Heaps of times. He just hadn't allowed it any space to plant itself down and mess with his head.

The house seemed cavernously cold and empty when he unlocked the front door. Like some abandoned Gothic mansion with clanging shutters and creaking floorboards, especially with the storm raging like a howling beast.

Blake closed the door against the wind and rain and bullets of hail but there were no wonderful cooking smells wafting through the air to greet him, no vases of fresh-smelling flowers on the hall table. The furniture he had bought with the house was just furniture. For all the comfort and welcome it gave, he could have been standing in an antiques warehouse. There were no excited barks from a mad dog with its paws scrabbling on the floorboards as it rushed at him in unmitigated joy at his arrival.

And worst of all...no Tillie.

Blake stood surrounded by the furniture and walls and roof of the house that was no longer a home. This was his prize. His Holy Grail. The mission he had spent years of his life dreaming of, planning, and working towards.

He had finally nailed it.

Why then did it feel so…pointless?

Blake walked into the sitting room, pulling back the curtains to look at the view over the lake and the old elm tree. The wind was thrashing the ancient limbs, shaking off leaves and twigs as if it cared nothing for the promise he had made all those years ago. But then he was almost blinded by an almighty flash of lightning, and then there was an ear-splitting crack of thunder followed by a splintering crash. He blinked to clear his gaze to see the ancient elm tree coming down like a felled giant.

Seeing that old tree lying there in such disarray forced him to take a good hard look at himself. The tree, once proud and strong and confident, was broken, battered, shattered. That tree had symbolised so much of his journey since childhood, but now it was worth little more than firewood and kindling.

How could Blake have got it so wrong? About this house? About his father?

About himself?

This property wasn't enough. This grand old house and all its memories were not enough. It wasn't making him feel satisfied. It wasn't making him feel anything but miserable. Lonely and miserable like an old house with furniture but no family.

His father was right, so too, wise old Mr Pendleton. What was a house without the one you loved sharing it with you?

Blake loved Tillie.

How could he have not realised that until now? Or maybe he had realised it. Maybe he had realised it from the moment he walked into that shop and encountered those sparkling nutmeg-brown eyes. But he had shied away from those feelings because it was too threatening to love someone who might not always be there.

But he'd lost her anyway.

Was it too late?

His heart felt as if it were crushed beneath the fallen ancient trunk of the elm tree. What if he'd blown his only chance with Tillie? He had let her walk away without telling her he loved her. He'd told her he didn't want a future with her, marriage and a family—all the things that had made this house the home it was meant to be.

But he did want those things.

He wanted them but only if he could have them with her.

Blake snatched up the keys, but on his way out

to his car he saw a bedraggled Truffles bolting up the driveway towards him. She shot through the front door and disappeared into the house leaving a trail of muddy footprints along the way.

He closed the front door and followed the dog to her hiding place behind the sofa in the sitting room. 'What are you doing here, girl?' he said, crouching down to soothe her. She shivered and shook and looked at him with the whites of her terrified eyes showing.

He took a throw rug off the nearest sofa and gently covered her with it to make her feel secure. He stood to close the curtains to keep the storm from frightening her, but then, over the sound of the storm outside, he heard the sound of a car coming up the driveway and his heart leapt.

'Stay,' he said to the dog.

Tillie saw Blake's car parked in front of the house and pulled up behind it, barely waiting long enough to turn off the engine. The first thing she'd noticed coming up the driveway was the elm tree was down.

Please God, don't let Truffles be under it.

Would the terrified dog have taken shelter under its over-arching limbs? She sprang out of the car and rushed through the pelting rain just as Blake opened the front door.

'Is Truffles here?' she asked. 'The elm tree is down. Please tell me she's here with you and not under it crushed to death. I can't find her anywhere and I can't bear telling Mr Pendleton she's—'

'She's here with me,' Blake said, taking her by the hands and bringing her inside the house and closing the door.

'Is she all right? Is she hurt? Is she—?'

'She's safe.' He took her by the upper arms. 'She's cowering behind the sofa in the sitting room but she's fine. Are you okay?'

Am I okay? Of course I'm flipping not okay.

Tillie closed her eyes to get control of her emotions. She should be feeling relieved about finding the dog safe but seeing Blake again was messing with her head and with her heart.

How long had Truffles been here? Why hadn't he called or texted to tell her the dog was okay? Surely it wouldn't have hurt him to do that?

But no, he didn't want anything to do with her now.

'I was so worried,' she said. 'She hates storms. I should have realised and gone back earlier to check on her and lock her in the cottage or something but the wind ripped the gate off the hinges and she must have escaped and the least you could have done is sent me a text to tell me she was all right.'

Blake's hands slid down to hers, giving them a reassuring squeeze. 'I was about to call you. Actually, I was on my way to see you.'

Tillie could feel his thumb moving over the diamond on her left hand. 'Oh, right, about the ring? I'm sorry I haven't got it back to you yet. I've tried heaps of times but it still won't budge. I'm going to get it cut off. I would have done it before this but it's been flat out crazy at the shop and—'

'I don't want you to give it back,' Blake said. 'I want it to stay right where it is.'

Tillie's heart was beating its way out of her ribcage like a pigeon fighting its way out of a paper bag. 'You don't mean that. You told me you didn't—'

'Don't remind me what a fool I've been, my darling,' he said. 'I love you. I want to marry you. I want to live with you and make babies with you. Please will you say yes?'

Tillie gazed up at him in stupefaction. 'Is… is this a joke?'

He gave a self-effacing chuckle. 'I suppose I deserve that. Of course it's not a joke. It's the truth. I love you and can't bear the thought of spending another day, another minute, another second without you. Marry me, darling. Let's fill this sad old house with love and laughter again.'

'But what about your father?' Tillie asked. 'Isn't he going to live here?'

'That was another thing I got totally wrong,' Blake said. 'He has other plans. He's finally moving on with his life and I couldn't be happier for him. He's met someone. Someone who means more to him, much more than this house and all the memories it contains.' He brought his hands up to cup her face, holding her gaze with his. 'You are my special someone, darling. The perfect someone I want to spend the rest of my life with.'

Tillie moistened her lips; still not certain she was actually hearing what he'd been saying. Surely she was dreaming. Surely this couldn't be real. He loved her? He really loved her? 'You keep calling me darling.'

His grey-blue eyes twinkled. 'I do, don't I? That's because that's what I am going to call you from now on. You are the love of my life. I think I realised it the first time I met you when I made you blush. But I was afraid of loving you. Scared of being vulnerable because I'd seen what loving someone so much had done to my father when my mum was taken away.'

Tillie put her hands against his chest; she could

feel his heart beating against her palm almost as fast as hers. 'I love you so much. I've missed you so much.'

'I've missed you, too,' he said. 'You have no idea how much. It's been like an ache deep inside. I haven't slept properly since you left. I keep reaching for you in the bed to find you gone.'

Tillie pressed closer to wind her arms around his neck. 'Do you really mean it? You really truly want to marry me?'

'Yes. As soon as it can be arranged,' he said. 'But if you can't bring yourself to get married in a church we could do it here. Down by the lake… although I think we might have to plant a new elm tree first.'

'That sounds like a great idea,' Tillie said, 'to symbolise a new beginning for McClelland Park.'

'So I take it that's a yes to my proposal?'

She gave him a teasing smile. 'Is this one for real or just pretend?'

He brought his mouth down to within reach of hers. 'This one's for real and it's for ever.'

EPILOGUE

One year later...

BLAKE CARRIED THE tea tray out to the garden of McClelland Park where Tillie was resting in the shade with Mr Pendleton. The new elm tree down by the lake wasn't quite big enough for shade yet, but every time he looked at it there in the distance, he thought of the future he was building with Tillie.

Blake's dad and Susie visited frequently and always enjoyed being there, but Jim Pendleton had been joining them just about every weekend ever since Blake and Tillie got back from their honeymoon. Jim loved seeing Truffles and he loved being around Tillie, but then, Blake had no argument with that. He loved being around her, too. More than words could ever say. More than he had thought it possible to love someone.

His life was so full and enriched by her. There was nothing he didn't enjoy about being married to her.

But in a few months' time he would have someone else to love. Tillie was just over twelve weeks pregnant and he couldn't believe how excited he was about becoming a father. She was glowing with good health, hardly any morning sickness so far and the only cravings she'd had were for him.

Tillie's Tearoom in the village in Maude Rosethorne's newly renovated cottage was doing brilliantly. Joanne and another assistant were doing a magnificent job of running things so Tillie could start to pull back a bit to prepare for motherhood. He was so thrilled she'd made the tearoom such a success because he liked to think it made up for all the disappointments she'd had before. Sure, he had helped her achieve it, but in so many countless ways she had helped and healed him.

Truffles was chasing a butterfly but came bounding over with her ears flapping when she smelt the scones and jam and cream Blake had set down. Some things never changed, but, hey, that was part of the joy of living with a nutty dog. Of being a family.

Blake sat down next to Tillie and placed his

arm around her waist, smiling down at her radiant face. 'Time to tell Jim our news, darling?' he said.

Tillie took Blake's hand and placed it on her abdomen. 'I have a feeling he's already guessed, right, Mr Pendleton?'

Jim Pendleton's face was wreathed in smiles. 'Congratulations. I couldn't be happier for you both and for McClelland Park.'

Blake looked at the new elm tree where it was anchoring its roots in the past and stretching its limbs into the future. He couldn't help feeling his mother would be happy the home she loved so much was going to be filled with joy and laughter once more.

He brought Tillie's hand up to his mouth and kissed the tips of her fingers, his heart swelling at the love reflected in her gaze. 'I think we should plant a new elm tree for each child we have. What do you think, darling?'

Tillie smiled. 'I think that sounds like a perfect plan.'

And it was.

* * * * *

#3573 THE GREEK'S FORBIDDEN PRINCESS
The Princess Seductions
by Annie West

Tragedy brings the press swarming around Princess Amelie, so she takes her nephew and runs to Lambis Evangelos for protection. His desire for Amelie is incredible, but he's always refused to taint her. Until Amelie's forbidden temptation arrives at his doorstep...

#3574 VALDEZ'S BARTERED BRIDE
Convenient Christmas Brides
by Rachael Thomas

The only way for Lydia to absolve her father's horrifying debts is to accept Raul Valdez's outrageous proposition. She must help him claim his inheritance—or marry Raul on Christmas Eve! Lydia finds she cannot resist her desire for the dark-hearted billionaire...!

#3575 KIDNAPPED FOR THE TYCOON'S BABY
Secret Heirs of Billionaires
by Louise Fuller

Nola Mason doesn't expect to see Ramsay Walker again after their explosive fling, never considering the consequences! Ram must claim his heir—he'll steal her away to his rain-forest hideaway and use their heat-fuelled passion to entice her into marriage!

#3576 A NIGHT, A CONSEQUENCE, A VOW
Ruthless Billionaire Brothers
by Angela Bissell

Emily Royce needs Ramon de la Vega's investment to save her business. But Ramon's piercing gaze reveals their potent chemistry—and one glorious night in Paris results in pregnancy! Ramon will make her his any way he can. Even with his ring!

YOU CAN FIND MORE INFORMATION ON UPCOMING HARLEQUIN® TITLES, FREE EXCERPTS AND MORE AT WWW.HARLEQUIN.COM.

HPCNM1017RB

Get 2 Free Books,
Plus 2 Free Gifts—
just for trying the Reader Service!

*When chauffeur Keira Ryan drives into a snowdrift, she and
her devastatingly attractive passenger must find a hotel...
but there's only one bed! Luckily, Matteo Valenti knows how
to make the best of a bad situation—with the most sizzling
experience of her life. It's nearly Christmas again before
Matteo uncovers Keira's secret. He's avoided commitment
his whole life, but now it's time to claim his heir...*

Read on for a sneak preview of
Sharon Kendrick's book
THE ITALIAN'S CHRISTMAS SECRET

One Night With Consequences

"Santino?" Matteo repeated, wondering if he'd misheard her.
He stared at her, his brow creased in a frown. "You gave him
an Italian name?"

"Yes."

"Why?"

"Because when I looked at him—" Keira's voice faltered as
she scraped her fingers back through her hair and turned those
big sapphire eyes on him "—I knew I could call him nothing
else but an Italian name."

"Even though you sought to deny him his heritage and kept
his birth hidden from me?"

She swallowed. "You made it very clear that you never
wanted to see me again, Matteo."

His voice grew hard. "I haven't come here to argue the
rights and wrongs of your secrecy. I've come to see my son."

It was a demand Keira couldn't ignore. She'd seen the brief
tightening of his face when she'd mentioned his child and
another wave of guilt had washed over her.

"Come with me," she said huskily.

He followed her up the narrow staircase and Keira was acutely aware of his presence behind her. She could detect the heat from his body and the subtle sandalwood that was all his and, stupidly, she remembered the way that scent had clung to her skin the morning after he'd made love to her. Her heart was thundering by the time they reached the room she shared with Santino and she held her breath as Matteo stood frozen for a moment before moving soundlessly toward the crib.

"Matteo?" she said.

Matteo didn't answer. Not then. He wasn't sure he trusted himself to speak because his thoughts were in such disarray. He stared down at the dark fringe of eyelashes that curved on the infant's olive-hued cheeks and the shock of black hair. Tiny hands were curled into two tiny fists and he found himself leaning forward to count all the fingers, nodding his head with satisfaction as he registered each one.

He swallowed.

His *son*.

He opened his mouth to speak but Santino chose that moment to start to whimper and Keira bent over the crib to scoop him up. "Would you...would you like to hold him?"

"Not now," he said abruptly. "There isn't time. You need to pack your things while I call ahead and prepare for your arrival in Italy."

"What?"

"You heard me. You can't put out a call for help and then ignore help when it comes. You telephoned me and now you must accept the consequences," he added grimly.

Don't miss
THE ITALIAN'S CHRISTMAS SECRET
available November 2017 wherever
Harlequin Presents® books and ebooks are sold.

www.Harlequin.com